YOU WERE WRONG

BY THE SAME AUTHOR

Jamestown
The Sleeping Father
Nothing Is Terrible
Stories from the Tube

YOU WERE WRONG

A Novel

Matthew Sharpe

BLOOMSBURY

New York   Berlin   London

Published by Bloomsbury USA, New York

All papers used by Bloomsbury USA are natural, recyclable products made
from wood grown in well-managed forests. The manufacturing processes
conform to the environmental regulations of the country of origin.

LIBRARY OF CONGRESS CATALOGING-IN-PUBLICATION DATA

Sharpe, Matthew
You were wrong : a novel / Matthew Sharpe.—1st U.S. ed.
p. cm.
ISBN 978-1-60819-187-1
I. Title.

PS3569.H3444Y68 2010
813'.54—dc22
2009052210

First U.S. edition 2010

1 3 5 7 9 10 8 6 4 2

Typeset by Westchester Book Group
Printed in the United States of America by Worldcolor Fairfield

To 2008

A house is a place to put boys and men.
—Marguerite Duras

. . . lamentable, lamentable, oh, lamentable!
—Henry James

ONE

AT TWENTY-SIX, Karl Floor had had a hard life: father dead, mother dead, stepdad sick and mean, siblings none, friends none, foes so offhanded in their molestations that they did not make a crisp enough focal point for his energies. Not that he had many energies—he had few. He wasn't born wan and slow, but misfortune made him so, and so he felt he would remain till death. Death: it cast a faraway light of exaltation over the future, as the prospect of a shining city on a hill gives comfort to pilgrims enduring a rough sea voyage, but he could not, as the pilgrims could not, *get there any faster.* He simply had to withstand storms and lulls, eat spoiled food, fall ill for months, never fully recover, and put up a sail at the first sign of wind. The strange woman in the upstairs hallway of his stepfather's house did not seem to him such a sign. He felt she was twenty-four. She wore jeans and a rose-colored T-shirt over her thin, strong body. She did not have on a mask, nor was she carrying any of his family's possessions, so Karl may be forgiven for not immediately identifying her as a burglar. A maid, he thought, an amateur from the university who'd tacked up posters around town with little half-cut tabs at the bottom that had her phone number on them that you could tear off and put in your pocket and call her later about daubing the inside of your house with her unwashed rag.

"Hi," she said.

Dust descended across the close air of the hallway on a mid-afternoon sunbeam that entered the house through a bedroom window to the right. The rose-colored T-shirt was lit by the beam, and now the words *fitness instructor* formed in his head.

"Are you—"

The likelihood of this afternoon's turning out to be other than grim was nil. His walk home from the high school where he taught math had been halted by the two worst boys from trig—a class of twenty pleasant sophomores and these two, seniors with no feel for trig or any subject that was not the idiot interruption of reasonable endeavor, or, to put it another way, they were assholes—*blond assholes*, he felt compelled to add. Karl himself was almost blond, and was willing to concede there were many blond people who were not assholes, and many brunettes and redheads who were, but a small, unkind segment of the blond population, he felt, acted out their unkindness as if wearing a blond wig, or as if they felt their blondness made them suitable for a role in which a brown-haired actor, no matter how brilliant the audition, would never have been cast. Steve McQueen and Faye Dunaway in *The Thomas Crown Affair*, McQueen laughing woodenly and kicking the air in the mod parlor of his mansion after pulling off a two-million-dollar bank heist, and Dunaway in her wide-brimmed hat crying out unconvincingly to the brown-haired chief of police, "Yes, I'm immoral, but so is the world!" That was who stopped Karl on his way home from school, a pair of high-society sophisticates with their own elite moral code, only both male, both teen, both crude, both dumb, both smelling like a week-old milk spill.

"Nice weather, Mr. Floor," one of them said, and the terrible thing was, it *was* nice weather, and the punching began.

A grown man, a teacher, beaten by two teens was grim. The central mathematical fact of the beating—*two* assailants—upset him most of all; five would've made it less personal; one would've given the dignity of a duel, or the randomness of an encounter with a lone psychopath; two made it intimate, a love triangle in which Karl was the odd man out.

"Are you—" he said to the burglar, forty minutes after the beating.

"Robbing you? Yes."

"Robbing *me*?"

"This is your house, isn't it?"

"Well, I live here."

"But it's not yours?"

"No."

"So you don't own anything here?"

"I didn't say that."

"Whose is it?"

"My stepfather's."

"Where's he?"

"At work."

"What's he do?"

"Manufacturing."

"Of?"

"Something vulgar."

"Toilet fixtures?"

"Not vulgar in that way, just not exalted."

"So everything in the world is either vulgar or exalted, with a line down the middle?"

"You're rude."

"I'm a robber."

They stood and assessed each other, the young man whose cuts congealed while his bruises bloomed, and the young woman who seemed to him in possession of a relaxedness that, had he been able to bring even his limited knowledge of human souls to bear on it, he'd have recognized as his own fantasy. They stood loosely sandwiched by the hallway's dark walls, the soft, low, beige carpet pushing up against their shoes. He saw that she was taking in his wounds while he was taking in her mouth, which, given the lips, took a long time: the softer the texture of the lip, and the fuller the saturation of the color red, the more seconds per square centimeter were required for accurate looking; they almost seemed Photoshopped in from a different face, possibly a somewhat larger one. He watched the little movements of this white and lovely face and felt—as he had often felt—that somewhere was written down all the combinations the forty-three face muscles could arrange themselves in, and the corresponding meaning of each, such that in any ten or fifteen seconds, a sentence could be read in someone's face by the person in command of the lexicon of physiognomy, and, in a minute, a paragraph, but Karl was not that person.

"What are you going to rob me of?"

"Still casing the joint," she said almost before he'd finished the question, but before that something had moved in her face that he'd have construed as dread had he been confident of his ability to construe. And maybe it wasn't a movement of her face but a feature of it, an asymmetry, a permanent imperfection that denoted weakness and caused him to see more and better in her than the fit and perfect-faced ass he'd initially written her off as, and to see, further, that he'd written her off as that partly because of his own present facial difficulties, i.e., typical him, he expected everyone today who impeded his progress from point A to point B to hurt him, morally if not also physically. Never mind that point B was his bed of unwashed sheets, and that little good had ever come of arriving there, since as nice as rest in that bed sometimes felt, at the end of it there was only ever unrest. And could a robber do other than improve the misery of this house he was bound to by a promise to a woman now dead?

"Excuse me," he said, and tried to walk past her down the hall. She didn't stop him but she didn't move. He was desperately afraid she would touch his face, or that he would touch hers. As he eased along the wall, his back shoved a small object to the ground. It lay in the carpet, a museum-quality mint-condition prototype of the widget his mother's sick and mean second husband oversaw the manufacture of, vacuum-sealed in lucite. They stared down at it. He felt what blood remained in his head pool against the inner lining of his face, and had the sensation that they were hanging on the wall while the widget, standing on the floor, observed them. Himself; his wounds; her; her T-shirt and strong arms; the suburban house with two floors, a basement, and an attic; a row of such houses, each with its half-acre of lawn, its tree, its beachhead of sidewalk; a whole town of these; many towns of these together and the big city whose gravity field fixed each in its orbit: all were prefigured and held in balance by the widget in the lucite void.

"Good night," Karl said, went to his room, lay down on grayish sheets, and slept.

"Hendrix at Monterey and Gustav Klimt's *The Kiss*?" she asked, looking at the posters on his walls. "How unimaginative. Wow, it smells like BO in here."

"How long was I asleep?"

"Ten seconds."

The brown window shades were drawn. The faux wood panels

were papered with the Klimt and Hendrix posters and a dozen others—genius rock bands and masterpieces of modern art that lost their luster through repetition in the bedrooms of a million young men on several continents.

"I feel sick," he said, as if this remark mattered.

She opened the shades. Light wedged into his eyes and pores. She sat on the edge of his bed and sighed. "Harrumph," he thought he heard her say. Her elbows rested on her knees and her two palms shared the weight of her chin; completing the circle, the elegant but somehow sad rounding of her back. "Yes, this problem is wearying and hard, let's consider it together," her posture seemed to say. No buttock but his own had touched his mattress lo these many years. Onto the very edge of his pillow he brought up a small taupe pool of half-digested food.

"Want some chamomile tea? It settles the stomach."

"Or you could get out of my room!" he said with more force than he'd said a thing in months.

From his vantage on the edge of the pillow farthest from the part of it he'd soiled, he saw the hair behind her left ear tautly pulled back by a redoubled scrunchie. The modest triangle of smooth skin between the back of her ear and the front of her pulled-back hair seemed especially vulnerable to his harsh opinion, and now he felt apologetic to this person whose posture on the edge of his bed looked like a lonely little question mark.

"You're right, of course," she sadly said, and stood up, and pulled the window shades back down, and left his room, the renewed darkness of which felt like the result of her having left it.

She walked back in with a damp washcloth so soft it had to have come from his stepfather's bathroom, not his own, and she moved toward him, washcloth held out like a weapon.

"Don't touch me with that thing."

"I'll hand it to you."

"Before you go rob my house?"

"Before I go rob your house."

The cloth was not just soft but warm: she'd taken the time to let the water from the spigot of his father's bathroom sink warm up before she'd held the cloth under it. Her game was very deep. She was gone again. He lay supine, the cloth in his left hand now wetting his left thigh. He disliked his thigh and his fate and this rich cloth that had been made a touch of cruelty by the girl who now banged around downstairs, maybe in the kitchen—the silverware, the microwave, the cuisinart—and would soon be but a memory.

He stared through the ceiling and into the attic above it, where the traces of those few bright moments of his boyhood—essays, paintings, a lumpy clay rabbit—lay entombed in dusty cardboard. She returned again, blowing on the steamy tea in the ancient mug, the old familiar green mug in hands so new and strange his mind could not quite make them hands—a hangnail, he saw, and redness, and faint chapped cracks.

"I think it's just this room that nauseated you," she said. "There's no air in here, there's, you know, moldy sock smell. Come to the living room."

"You're inviting me to my living room?"

"Yes."

His strategy with this mysterious woman would be to go with her to the living room and slowly drink the tea she made him and tell her anything she wanted to know.

"Isn't this nicer?" she said, on a stuffed chair.

"What's your name?"

"Sylvia Vetch."

The front door of the house stood open, as did the kitchen door in the back. A fresh spring breeze came through. This room did seem unusually nice to him, throbbing head and nausea to one side. Evidently one's house had to be violated to be nice, doors flung back, the difference between outside and inside reduced, strangers and breezes coming in; nicer still, perhaps, if the windows were smashed. He looked at her with his right eye while he allowed the left side of his face to roll along the soft, creased, tan leather couch's back, gazing with his left eye down into the crevice below, the dark unknown region where dwelt pocket change, office supplies, remote controls of old, whole sandwiches of crumbs, decades of dust.

"I guess I'll start robbing you now."

"Do you want to know my name?"

"No."

"It's Karl Floor."

"You're giddy."

"I got beat up."

"I see."

"How do you know? Maybe I was in a car accident."

"Were you?"

"No. What will happen if I try to stop you from robbing me?"

"I'll beat you up."

He lightly vomited again, into the crevice. An umber waterfall inundated the land beneath the couch's cushion that time forgot but vomit remembered.

He had been holding the tea and now put it down on the glass top of the coffee table. Sylvia Vetch sat still and watched him from her chair with eyes of an almost hostile shade of blue, her strong and elegant arms resting on the chair's arms, her hands clutching them, tapping them, their movements betraying an agitation whose cause Karl knew was relevant to him but was too sad and dumb to figure out.

"Why are you just sitting there?" he said.

Again a wave of something like distress passed through her. "I don't know."

"Figuring out what you're going to take?"

"Yes."

"Want help?"

"Taking things?"

"Deciding."

"Okay."

"Well, people who are acting in a play always say, 'What's my character's motivation?'"

"But I'm *not* acting."

"What are you, stupid?"

"No!" Her face turned red; she stood up, walked toward the door, walked back with hands out as if to strangle Karl, sat down, and looked at him in supplication. This business of eyes, their meanings, their requests, their acts of aggression, their penetrations of the skin, the flesh—astonishing.

"Then why are you burglarizing my house in the middle of the day, with me in it?"

"What's your point?"

"My point is, what's your motivation for being here?"

"I don't have to tell you." She leaned forward and down in her chair as if she, too, would now be sick.

"I'm asking so I can help you figure out what to take, remember?"

"Oh. Well then. My—uh—motivation is to—God, this is so stupid, who told you people know their own motivations? Not all life is math, you know, where each question has its answer."

"Why did you say that?"

"What?"

"That life isn't math."

"Because you're a math teacher."

"I didn't tell you I'm a math teacher."

Her white face went red and she stood up. "I've got to go."

"Sit down!" He did not remember ever speaking to someone like this, even a student, and he felt his words go into her the way her look had gone into him more than once this afternoon.

She did not sit down, and he was no longer sitting up. He lay sideways toward the front of the couch, looking up at her as she looked down at him across the low, rectangular, glass-top table with its vintage beer-ad coasters, its stack of books of antique art. He watched the workings of her lungs move her rose T-shirt up and down. Her knees were bent, her arms were bent and tensed, a karate sort of stance she seemed to have leapt into from a sleep interrupted by a stranger's touch.

"I want a buffer between me and, you know, nothing," she said.

"What are you talking about?"

"Why I'm robbing you."

"Oh, well, God, I want *no* buffer between me and nothing."

"Only someone raised in Seacrest could say that. Have you ever wandered over the line into Centraldale, where I'm from? Not everyone lives in a beautiful two-story house with a big front lawn. Have your parents ever been unemployed?"

"They've been dead."

"You just roll along through the hours, don't you, living in this house for free, storing up your teacher's pension against your last day, as if you could kill time without doing harm to your own life."

"You don't know anything about me!" Karl said, though everything this Sylvia had just said about him was true. "Fine," he said, "if you're going to leave, leave. Just don't stay here and lie to me."

She looked at him awhile, was scrutinizing him, was—if it were possible he was not mistaken—sizing him up in advance of telling him, finally, something true about herself. "There are forces in this world, my dear friend, darker than I think you're willing to imagine could ever touch your life."

"Oh, I can imagine. Two of the 'forces' touched my face about an hour ago." Even as he said this he knew those were not the forces she meant. He sensed that the piece of information in her remark most relevant to him was *my dear friend*, which affected him as the sequel of something whose beginning he was already supposed to know. "Dark forces?" he said. "Who are you, Princess Leia?"

Something agitated her excessively.

"Tell me who you are!"

"I can't! Not yet."

"Why not *yet*?"

She reached out with both hands as if to gather back into her body the words she'd just said. "Forget it. There's no *why* because there's nothing to tell."

"There's a safe in the study with jewels and cash."

"What?"

"You're robbing me, remember?"

"Do you know the combination?"

"No. There are things in boxes in the attic."

"What things?"

"A rabbit."

"What kind?"

"Of clay, that I made, as a kid, or didn't make. Another kid made it, and I made one too, but when they came out of the kiln mine was misshapen and his was beautiful. His was the shape and color—blue, various blues—I'd meant to make mine and thought I'd made mine. I refused to believe I'd made mine, I said I'd made his, and believed that, and cried. This all happened at school. The teacher insisted I take mine home, I said I wouldn't, I said it was only fair I take his, which I thought was mine. This other kid, Mike Schoen, who was stronger than I was and handsomer and nicer and more generous and had better grades and a better rabbit, said, 'It's all right, I'd like him to have it,' or some magnanimous speech like that. He ceded me his rabbit. He didn't say, 'This nicer rabbit really is his,' he needed to let the teacher and me know that he was giving up his rabbit for me. The cocksucker."

"And you want me to take this rabbit."

"Yes."

"Why?"

"It isn't mine anyway."

"What should I do with it?"

"Give it back to Mike Schoen."

"I don't know him."

"You will, you'll find him and give him his rabbit and marry him, you two will put the rabbit on your mantel."

"I don't want the stupid rabbit."

"It's not stupid, it's my finest accomplishment."

"Why are you helping me rob your house?" she said in a tone that amounted to a confession that she was not robbing it, if Karl was to be trusted to decipher what tones amounted to.

"It's burdensome to me," he said.

"Why?"

"I own it."

"I thought you said your mean stepfather owns it."

"I didn't say he was mean, what makes you think that?"

"Look at you."

"He's not the one who beat me up."

"Yes, but you're the sort of person who gets beaten up because he has a mean stepfather, which, as a grown man, you should get over."

"Only people with happy childhoods have free will," he said. "I own this house with him. My mother, when she was dying—"

"How old were you?"

"Sixteen. She asked me to stay with him and care for him."

"Why?"

"He's sick."

"Your mother asked you to live here and look after him until he dies, in exchange for which you will own the house and any other assets in her estate."

"How did you know that?"

"I'm intuitive. Why does it happen that the dying person extracts some untenable promise from the living person, and this always happens with the dying person lying in bed and the living person sitting in a chair, and the dying person hates the living person for living, so much that she's going to cast a pall over the living person's life by making him do something for a long time that he doesn't want to do, and the living person agrees to it as if that'll make the dying person somehow not die? This is just bad faith on both people's parts."

"Get out of my house!"

"Well, I wish you wouldn't yell at me, it's hurtful."

Was that a tear in her eye? "I truly hate that you're in my house and I'm drinking this tea you made me. Whatever awful thing you're going to do to me, I wish you'd do it already because the anticipation is increasingly worrisome and unpleasant."

TWO

THE FRONT WINDOWS OF HIS CAR were down and
Sylvia Vetch stuck her feet out the passenger side. She'd rolled her
jeans above her knees. Her calves and shins were beautifully un-
haired, pale and shinily moisturized against the cracked beige vinyl
of the old Volvo door's inner wall. Karl Floor drove them down a
road in his town near the coast, the lush scent of swamp grass
in the air, dust, dunes, tiny seashells brittle and bleached, the old
engine's moribund racket, its unwholesome light gray exhaust, a
poem of going to the beach. The upstairs TV wobbled in the center of the backseat. The smaller stolen items on its left and right
seemed to pray to it. The cracked-open parts of Karl's face slowly
came together. His wounds were not so bad. He didn't know how
bad they were. He didn't know how bad these last few hours were,
in the small scheme of his own happiness, the very clinging to
which had thus far in his life brought about its opposite, so screw
caution and the knowledge that this woman was acting on behalf
of a goal or person or principle to which or to whom he was
probably an impediment, and that what she intended was inimical
not only to his happiness but also to his material comfort and
physical health. He wanted her, there, he wanted her, in so many
words. He did not want her *for* anything—sex, children, lifelong

companionship, to be shattered by. He drove nowhere with her for nothing.

Imagine, then, their arrival, after a hard hour on a gorgeous beach, at a house physically compromised by neglect, painted wood-color by beach weather. A party or something like it may have been under way. "This is Stony," someone said. "This is Rich, John, Jen, Jan, Tom, Rob, Arv." Karl's head was a mass of uncooled lava held together by a soft yellow hat. Stony, someone with long hair about thirty years old—Karl liked to establish a person's numbers in case this would make up for the not-knowing of which he seemed to possess a greater amount than most—led him by the hand from one room to the next. They were two men holding hands at a loud party in a messy house, Stony's hand large and dry and strong, palm somehow curved away from Karl's and representing knowledge about Stony Karl would never have. They arrived at a sturdy metal vat of beers. "Have one."

"Can't."

"Why?"

"My head."

"Mine." Stony pointed at his: his long and thick and gently wavy chestnut hair, of which far more care had been taken than of this house, hung partway down his white long-sleeved button-down shirt, which he wore untucked, and which was more than just a normal business shirt, who knew how? To his face there was a lined handsomeness almost on a par, though it creeped him out to think of it, with the smooth loveliness of that of Vetch.

Karl drank beer from a brown bottle in a room he understood by its rotting-broccoli smell to be the kitchen, with a grimy and sticky linoleum floor that people his age with more talent for nesting—Karl had been to their homes—would have spent days pulling up to reveal the valuable old hardwood floor beneath. Tipping the bottle and his poor enormous head back, he leaned against a counter's edge and found a horizontal line of unknown wet transferred to the back of his cotton chino pants just below the lonely belt loops. He was comforted by the rank dishevelment of the house, but not by the ugly unimaginativeness of his own clothes as he now abruptly perceived them in contrast to those of Stony, though he did enjoy his own yellow hat. Dance music to be known by the masses a few months hence came softly from another room.

"Has he tried the goulash?" That was Arv, he thought (twenty-eight), who had appeared along with Jen. Sylvia Vetch was gone.

"Don't give him the goulash, give him the *dentice*," Stony said, "which I adapted from a recipe by Nigella Mantovani, though mine is more authentic because I understand the pared-down purity of true southern Italian cooking. You have to start with excellent ingredients of an extreme freshness."

"The *dentice*! Oh, the *dentice*!" said Arv, whose haircut and clothes, like Karl's, were wrong for the room, and whose face was like putty with air holes, but Arv came on strong now with his impression of an Italian accent—of a whole Italian person, fingers bunched and moving rhythmically beneath his chin, loving the *dentice*. "Is-a so fresh, the fish, she is-a caught this-a morning in-a the river behind-a my grandafadda his-a house. He caught-a with-a his-a own-a hand-a. No sauce. No oil. No pan. In-a Milano they put-a the sauce is-a stupid-a sauce a rich-a man he make-a the sauce. No. My grandafadda he no shit-a on-a the *dentice* widda sauce. *Mangia*."

Arv was sweating, his shoulders hunched. Stony had a relaxed posture and elongated neck. He didn't do accents and didn't need to. He stood still in composed silence and said with only the contraction of a few eye muscles that he took the mockery as a form of violence he would feel justified in responding to with his own far more severe violence, one memorable enough to dissuade Arv or anyone from mocking him ever again.

And somehow Karl ate a whole fish that was bland and contained an odd, bitter nonfish taste he knew would cause him trouble of an unusual kind.

He swooned. He didn't know he'd swooned. "Someone had blundered," someone said, either inside of Karl or not inside of him.

"Let's take a tour of the house." Arv had him by one arm and Stony painfully by the other, evidently Vetch surrogates, the former hairy, the latter smooth. Where was Vetch? She had abandoned him. His goose was cooked. "This is this room," Stony said, back in a room Karl had passed through on his way to the beer an hour ago or more—seventy-five minutes, approximately, or ninety. Three long, faded floral couches, cushions lastingly depressed, stood side by side by side against a wood-paneled wall like the wall Karl had at "home." People Karl's age sat on them, stood on them, bounced on them, lay on them, one's head on another's leg. The music was louder now. Other people, also mostly young, danced or stood on the room's patchwork of soggy, ancient, indoor-outdoor carpeting. "And this is *this* room," Arv said as they all three stepped down into a slightly sunken octagon with a parquet floor whose design they said was a secret sign. "Don't touch the candle on the floor in the center of the star." This room was speckled with people, sitting with drinks or laughing faceup on the floor. One of them was almost her but turned out not to be at the last second. Karl's—"Karl's"—TV was in there too, on a shelf on a wall at the height of his eyes. Stony, Arv, and Karl were on the TV, the backs of their heads were, as seen from above. Karl turned to see the camera above and behind him, didn't, and turned back to see the back of his head, turning back. "Someone had blundered," someone said again, not Stony, not Arv, and Karl looked around for Stony's eyes. He was dizzy thanks to fish, fists, Vetch, her men—he thought of them as hers—her party, its music, its crowd and their smells, the expressionistic dilapidation of the house. Stony's eyes found Karl's, on the way up the two steps out of the octagonal room. The left side of Karl's left eye still registered the dull and pulsing glow of his own TV at the moment he became aware that Stony's eyes now held his own more forcefully than his hand had been holding Karl's arm a moment before. His face, up close and still, was not as uniformly tan as it had seemed in motion and at a remove. He was older than Karl had thought. The creases in his face and shifts in hue seemed not to be accidental but crafted by Stony, confirming a remark Karl had heard that at a certain age a man had to take charge of his own face. Arv was funny, voluble, and loud, but Stony in his quietude shone with an aggressive personal luster, and now, without touching Karl, assaulted him. Karl was looking too, but Stony was looking more. Stony used not just his eyes but his nostrils, mouth, and pores to look into Karl. Who was Stony? How could he do this? God should not have put the face on the human body where He did; it would have been more useful, less in danger of violation if placed elsewhere, in many locations, perhaps. The face's parts should not all have been bunched in one spot but dispersed: the mounting of so many crucial sense organs nearly on top of one another made the face the lone cosmopolis in the body's attenuated nation of volcanoes, deserts, and small farms. The conversation of the pairs of eyes went on, but Stony's eyes wouldn't let Karl's eyes talk. Stony's filibustered, shouted their interrogation. Karl was more disheartened by what Stony's eyes were doing to his soul than by what his students' fists had done to his face. He knew the particular way that this vigorously not-nice man was looking at him had to be connected to the reason the man's beautiful friend had materialized in his house that afternoon.

And then he didn't know anything, including where he was, geographically or otherwise, nor could he calculate the angle of his body to the earth. "Someone had blundered," and she was upon him, but not in *that* way. More in a health care way, mental health care, but straddling him in mental health care, riding him in emergency mental health care, concerned, rhythmic resuscitation in rose-colored T-shirt and rolled-up jeans, on a forest path perhaps, with light, soft sticks beneath and a latticework of leaves above, black against the purple sky, and others nearby, in pairs, and similar in form: one down, the other up; one sick, the other not; one extracting promises the other could not keep.

THREE

TWENTY THOUSAND YEARS after a slab of ice the size of France had made the beach he now woke up on in sodden clothes, Karl assessed the feel of having had all but a thin crust of flesh, hair, and skin scraped out of him by Stony and whatever series of people and events—now compressed into a red, wet bolus of vague sense memory—had come after Stony in the night. The beach and Karl were alike in being relatively young yet colonized, built upon, much used, depleted, and temporary. Where was his hat? Someone had stolen his hat. An individual or group of individuals had absconded with his head covering. A man of Karl's light skin and facial challenges would do well to have something useful on his head of a late spring day, and he had done a good job of keeping his on his on the whole trip till now—well, not till now but till a time between his last moment of knowing he had it and now, and he hoped that moment would be returned to him just as he hoped his hat would, especially as the location of the two—time and hat— likely were connected. The hat was soft and of a faded yellow that could not have been arrived at by manufacture. The brim was stiff enough to keep the sun off, but not so stiff as to jut militarily ahead of him into the world. The band had an orange tartan pattern unrelated to Karl's people, who were from the Balkans. The whole effect was of an inoffensively monstrous and immortal daffodil. Where was his hat? Where was the house? Where was a car, a road, a tree to give him shade? Where was Karl himself? Sitting, not yet ready to stand, on a hot beach with low and mostly dead scrub brush, the horizon either distant or obscured. Dead brown sea things had been cast up everywhere on the shore, a rough night for the beach as for Karl. What was his shoe situation? Moistened and sand-filled.

"Dude!" someone said—Arv, he deduced. Till now, Karl had hoped one of the modest consolations of being a pariah would be to complete life never having been called "dude." "I've got gatorade." Arv put the jar to Karl's lips. The substance's sugary disgustingness flooded him, ran down his chin and onto his chest, where its bright and indelible dye made a stain on his off-white shirt. "Don't be uptight about the shirt": Arv. Arv's face right now, all up in Karl's, unknowingly explained to Karl why anyone would ever want to punch anyone's face. And yet however it might simplify one's life to do so, one could not discount even Arv. Did not the row of retail shops on Main Street kneel for Arv as for all humanity after two shots of tequila at The Dinghy? He now walked too fast along the beach, squat, furry, curly-haired, hunching forward into life, feet splayed at right angles when he took each step as if they had argued and would go their separate ways.

"Would you please slow down, Arv?" Arv smelled, no worse than Karl, but Arv had slept indoors. "Where are we going, Arv?"

"People like to put it at the end like that with that little freefloating sarcasm, 'Where are we going, *Arv?*' like my name itself is the punch line of a joke." Arv in his quotation had made his face look beat up à la Karl and had done well too with Karl's high and

reedy voice. "People think I'm just a clown," he said, and reprised
last night's *dentice* performance.

"Rough night?" Karl asked.

"The usual. How about you?"

"I don't know."

"So you always do that?"

"Do what?"

Arv smiled. "It's all right, no one gets to stop being lonely without being violated. Breakfast?"

"I don't see a building anywhere."

"See that parking lot over there, and that car?"

He saw his own old golden Volvo, abandoned, door open, on a
small patch of sandy black asphalt. "Did I leave that there like
that?"

"No."

"You're driving my car now?"

"We're pretty communal, down at the House. Maybe you're
not ready to be one of us yet but you sure acted like it last night.
Do you find *Volvo* has a dirty ring to it?"

" 'The House'? 'One of us'? Is this a cult?"

Arv laughed and slapped Karl's shoulder three times. Karl felt
fraternal sympathy with someone who, not sure how to be a man,
hoped the use of manhood's physical forms would help.

Arv pulled him along toward the car. "Sylvia told us about your
situation. Maybe we can help you with it."

"What situation?"

"You still look thirsty. You want some water?"

"Yes, please."

Arv gave him a mauve and translucent plastic water jar whose
screw top was attached to its neck by a bendable plastic armature,

as children's mittens are attached to their coat sleeves. The jar looked to be communal and of questionable cleanliness. Karl thought of pouring the water into his mouth so the jar wouldn't touch his lips, but drank the normal way. "What situation?"

"You know, the house you live in."

"My house?"

"Ownership is burdensome."

"Have you ever owned anything?"

"Yes."

"I'm not talking about a toothbrush." As he said this, it occurred to him with horror that these people shared a toothbrush.

"I was once in danger of owning something big that my parents were going to give me," Arv said, "but I successfully avoided it."

"How did you avoid it?"

"By being disowned."

"Why?"

"The usual reason middle-class parents disown their son. Have some more water."

"I'm good." Karl was not good. Sand was deep in the gelatinous fabric of his facial scabs. His cranium was a helmet of bone two sizes too small for his brain. His shoes chafed, his legs ached as if he'd run all night, his back was in knots, he smelled like anchovies and rotting pineapple. They arrived at his car.

"You want to drive?" Arv said.

"You're asking me if I want to drive my own car?"

"If you like."

"You drive it."

Karl lay faceup in the far back of the Volvo station wagon. His knees were bent and his head rested uncomfortably in the angle made by the back of the backseat and the back inner wall of the car on the driver's side. Arv was a terrible driver—people often are in other people's cars—but Karl couldn't be bothered to voice his thoughts on this fact, or notice it. Jouncing along above the soft and pitted beachfront road, Karl gazed up at the treetops and the clouds. A cloudy day. Whom did he love best, his mom, his dad, his sis, his bro? He had no mom, no dad, no sis, no bro. His friends? He hadn't heard the word. His home? He'd never been home. Money? He hated it as he hated God. What, then, did he love? He loved the clouds . . . the passing clouds . . . up there . . . up there . . .

Squared-off building tops cut into the sky. The Shadow's Rest Motel, the Spy Store, piano store, billiard hall, wireless shop for all your wireless needs, paper goods, check cashing, dry cleaning, furniture, jewelry, dresses, drugs, ice cream, produce, pizza, day care, gas, law: a town.

Arv parked at the gas station, whose cashier stood on the far side of an old screen door light on its hinges in a one-story building with a half-peeled-off green paint job. They passed the cashier and entered a dark room with small café tables. Half a dozen big and lazy flies cycled one by one in and out of hearing range and view. Voices from the darkness called Karl's name. "It's alive!" someone said who must have been Stony.

And then her form swam in from the gloom. She wore a different shirt today, of a blue taken from the sky he'd seen from the car, and pants of black, softer than before, and flip-flops, dirty toes exposed, chipped black polish on the nails. He knew faces could say more than their owners knew and he wanted her face to tell him what he didn't have the words to ask her. The face of Vetch in the semidark, its soft white nostrils, their one or two blown capillaries, the roseate glow, blue eyes obscured even when the lids were up, an understated choker at her neck holding up a stone or coin; would she speak to him? He liked her better nervous; she didn't seem so now.

"Vetch," he said.

"How's the burglary, Floor?"

"Up yours."

"So he *does* remember what he did last night," Arv said.

She looked at Arv as if he were an additional fly. There was the unsettled question of whether her intentions toward Karl were mean or nice, whose answer would not influence his feelings, only their consequences. He sat in an old-fashioned folding chair of metal frame and wooden slats, also painted green, also peeling, as was the round table. Two of the others, Jen and Rich, he felt, were there. He did not at first hear the conversation, but listened to the music of the initiates' understated mirth.

"Karl needs a big breakfast," Stony said, after a time. How did everything he said sound like an insult?

"My wallet is gone." He was not sure if he'd just discovered this or had known it for some time.

"Your credit is good here."

Karl looked at Sylvia, who said, "We didn't take your wallet!"

Stony, who always looked as if he'd just been given a massage, said, "Don't yell at Karl, he's in pain," and went to order Karl his food. Arv, handicapped with eyebrows and a mouth formed for wit, excused himself, as did Rich and Jen, if that's who they were. Sylvia stood up as well. Karl positioned himself in his chair to say the words "Don't go," but couldn't make them come.

"Come with me," she said. He went, tethered to mistrust, out into a luminous garden behind the gas station, and then into a woods behind that, unremembered pleasure still half-wheeling in his brain. He had drunk of potent wines last night, and perhaps had found himself for an hour among the valiant of voluptuousness. He walked in this small, wild forest, Sylvia strong and thoughtful at his side. A vise clamped down on his own thoughts, and tightened.

"Cat got your mouth?" she said.

"Where are you taking me?"

"To the house."

"What about breakfast?"

"It will be delivered. Jen runs the café today."

"Who runs it other days?"

"Jan, or Rich, or Steve, or me, or—"

"What is your purpose?"

"I don't understand the question."

"What is the purpose of you, this group, what are you?"

"What are *you*?"

"What were you doing in my house?"

"Man, Floor, would you cut it out? I like you, you're . . . odd, and . . . sad. Look at your hair. Come here a sec."

They stood in the dark forest, the sun far away. A little chestnut bird flew by while others, in the trees, sang a melancholy song. Salt air cooled their skin and they shivered. Again her pale face glowed, absent an explicable light source, and her full, soft lips came toward him while staying still. She reached out a hand and he stepped back.

"Hold still."

"What are you doing?"

"Fixing your hair."

"Is it broken?"

"Karl!"

"Don't touch my face."

"I won't."

She fixed it, yanked it a little, her unruly boy.

"Now," she said, "I'd like to hug you."

"Why?"

"No reason."

"No."

"How about if I touch your shoulders with my hands?"

"That would be worse."

"Why?"

"Then you would look at me."

"So?"

"I'm ugly."

She hugged him fast and tight, careful to avoid his face. He stood trembling with his arms at his sides.

"Now hug me back."

"I'm scared."

"Please."

He put his hands on her back. She trembled too. Her cool and salty shirt, her strong and nervous muscles underneath: two humans touching at the bottom of the forest, glued together by the shadows of the trees.

He did not know how long his eyes had been closed, nor why he opened them then. It appeared first as a white speck, emerging from the green gloom as a vengeful beast might rise up from the bottom of the sea to break apart the most concentrated act of solace he had known to date. "You've tensed up again," she said, and pressed a place inside his shoulder blade that caused him therapeutic pain. The speck became a shirt and pants and shoes, all white. No face yet but the angry and ill-meaning one he gave it, this thing that came toward them with no real body but temporary plasma materializing inside the white clothes with the malevolent seductiveness of visual beauty. "Help me, please," he thought he heard her say, and the thing that came toward them on the forest floor was Stony, loping up with a breakfast made for Karl himself inside an oblong white styrofoam takeout box that dangled from the crook of this man's first two fingers in a thin white plastic sack. Thus ended the hug. What could ever be the meaning of Stony for Karl? It worried him. Our friend was on the side of humanity that would always take things hard, and knew that this new lady in his life, though she might keep him for a time, would grow weary of this burden of how he took things. He did not see, or saw but did not know, that she was his kindred and not just in this.

The three of them walked on. He sensed Stony imagined himself the rearward of two aristocrats carrying a peasant to breakfast on a platform and therefore being given only the peasant's back to contemplate, enjoying the novelty of voluntary servitude and not enjoying the servitude.

Emerging from the woods, Karl saw the house in the light for the first time, from the back. It was dug into a steep hill whose lower end the three of them were leaning into. There was a short ascending meadow of weeds between the woods and house. An open back porch with pale gray dirty concrete floor greeted them. Grass grew in its cracks. Bicycles, balls, garden tools, croquet mallets and stakes and hoops were strewn on it. There was a wheelbarrow and a green hose, and there were dead plants in small black plastic pots on the windowsills. Gray round poles rose up from the concrete floor and supported the back of the house. The second-story window frames had once been given a coat of green paint of which only fragments now were left.

"What's with all the green?"

"That's our color," she said.

"Whose?"

"Ugh, you're so literal."

Karl tried to imagine a perfect world in which one would always only be hugged by Sylvia Vetch, or in which all experience would have the tenor of a Vetch hug. Could "Ugh, you're so literal" have been a verbal hug of the painful kind that liberated toxins from deep within him toward the ultimate goal of free energy flow through the body and extended pain-free living? Perhaps, if someone had not blundered.

"Karl's coming, everyone!" someone said from the screened-in deck above the back porch. He wasn't sure this was the same house as last night. "Don't look!" he was instructed as he went in through the screen door of the back porch and was led up a dark stair, but how could one not look? A pizza stain on the wall and a tube sock, once white, pasted to the banister with mold, were but two ocular sensations. And if one had somehow been able not to look, one would still have felt and heard underfoot the squishy nubs of basement carpet that denoted an undealt-with flood, and one would still have smelled—well, it was complicated, grim, and didn't have a name he knew.

"Don't go in the kitchen!"

He saw a shoe, a leg, heard a bracelet jangle in a hall. They scurried away from him like talking cartoon mice. And this was also the dream of a certain kind of person, that the meaning which animated the world was in constant flight just ahead of his arrival, leaving behind the mute and inchoate objects it had vacated, like the ones that covered the dining room table on which a grimy place had evidently been cleared for him. On both chair and light tan tabletop dust adhered to spots where syrup or other sticky gunk had not been fully wiped up. Nothing anywhere in this house had been fully wiped up. And here was that seemingly random cluster of objects on the table and adjacent chairs, the puzzle adequate time would not be given him to solve: newspapers and magazines and books, plastic trays of dried fruits, antacids, laxatives, and analgesics, a combination lock, pliers, water bottles, SPF 30, keys, a watch, a phone and its unsnapped holster, scissors, CDs, pens, a flashlight, half-full coffee cups topped with hieroglyphs of milk, someone's calendar and checkbook, a canister of compressed air promising to "quickly blow harmful dust & dirt from delicate or hard-to-reach surfaces." A hand placed the sealed styrofoam takeout tray before him, opened it, and retreated. There were his cold and solid scrambled eggs, there a cooled-down, hardened slice of toast. He looked up. No one was about and yet he felt peered at, a bad actor on a meticulously trashed stage set, performing a scene in which a confused solitary man eats takeout eggs, which had been and would be performed all morning and for days to come by men throughout the length and breadth of the landmass. The relation between the morning meal and the house it happened in, between house and land, land and meal, could be expressed in a formula consisting of numbers, letters, symbols, and a single equal sign; the lifespan of one man might simply not have been sufficient time to derive the formula. Perhaps he'd know it at ninety, were he unlucky enough to live to that age, though surely it would not matter to him then. Truths harder to bear than the ones he could conceive of now would dominate his thoughts at that time, should that time come. Life presented a set of intractable problems that rose up and fell away in an unrelenting series, or maybe it was the same problem in different forms, or in the same form but seen differently as the organism first grew and then decayed. Sometime in the last twenty-four hours Karl had crested, and now joined those trudging down the slope into the valley of the dead.

The suck of the sticky wooden floor on the bottoms of Sylvia's flip-flops announced her arrival. She presented herself, hands on hips. The bare skin of her arms, neck, and face, sensing Karl's gaze upon them, changed hue. The skin, he felt, after the clitoris, is the most sensitive organ of a woman's body.

"We've been given the kitchen," she said.

"In what sense?"

"To clean."

"Why now, after all these years?"

Her answer was to reverse the direction of the looking, so that now he felt his skin warm beneath the heat of her eyes.

"You and me, hon, cleaning the kitchen."

"I'd like to nap first."

"You'll nap when you're dead."

"Maybe not."

They stood in the kitchen and assessed their task. The pathways of the blue linoleum floor most traveled by were least begrimed, but not by much. Papers, bread crumbs, scuff marks, and well-worn plant pulp had insinuated themselves into the lowest tier of the kitchen landscape. No surface, horizontal, vertical, or otherwise, was without its trace of hard and absentminded use. They looked at the sink and adjacent countertops and decided that the teetering mountain range of dishes, pots, and pans—coated with food and with what happens to food when let to sit in warm moist air for a month or more—would be their first task. They cleared away an area of floor, covered it with newspaper, moved things from the sink and placed them there. They hosed and scrubbed the sink and countertops. The muscles of his arms, neck, and back ached. She gave him aspirin and water of questionable provenance. They scoured and hosed, soaped and rinsed. Without speaking of it, they divided the tasks and agreed upon a high standard of cleanliness, nothing less than which would justify the difficulty and grossness of what they were doing. The pile diminished slowly therefore. They had created a wide swath of countertop on which things could be dried by the air, but they hadn't yet cleared a place for them to be stored, and a quick opening and closing of cabinet doors had revealed that this, too, would be a task requiring considerable time, energy, and thought. The orderly distribution of objects in a home had long troubled Karl; it had been done wrong in all the homes he'd visited, not to speak of the highly problematic one he lived in. He himself had never been in charge of this unavoidable feature of domestic life, and the possibility of undertaking it with Sylvia Vetch exhilarated him. In inventing a new design for object positioning, and therefore also for the way bodies move through homes, they would remake the very concept of *home*, and remake the possibilities for boy-girl contact and connection. It was possible, it was possible to become someone new in this way, not just new to oneself but new to the world, to bring into the human sphere feelings that had not existed before, made from scratch with care by two gentle souls who admired each other and had similar values, though not, of course, identical values, because it was in the happy friction of values that the serious pleasure of relationship was felt and new things were created.

As they journeyed deeper into work, sweat soaked his skin, hair, and clothes. His fragrance, fluid added, ripened and intensified. His pains had eased off and were now joined in his body by the spirit of work. Sylvia did not in any way that he could detect express her dislike of his smell, if she felt one. And if she herself was the source of any smells they were masked by Karl's own and by the pungent lime and ammonia of household detergents. Even in smell she remained closed to him.

"So who owns this house?" he asked.

"Who owns your house?"

"I already told you."

"Well, but think about it. The thing you said, it don't make sense."

"What did I say?"

"About your mother."

"Remind me."

"On her deathbed."

"Oh, right, the death of my mother, which you mocked."

They stood side by side at the sink. Each scrubbed a pot. She reddened, tensed, and paused. "I didn't mock it, you misunderstood me."

He turned to her, startled. "Just at the moment when a little sensitivity is required, like when the subject is the death of a man's mother, you start throwing punches."

"And when life throws a punch at you, you cower, saying, 'Don't hit me, my mother died.'"

They faced each other, mouths open. "You don't know me well enough to say that."

"I know. I'm sorry. I don't know why I said that."

He scrutinized her face for something unequivocally true.

"You're right though," she said. "I wasn't, uh—"

"I know. Shut up."

She giggled, first giggle of heretofore mirthless Vetch; a wave of joy in sad and sweaty Karl.

"But," she said, "you said your mother said you had to stay in your house and take care of your stepfather until he died and then you would inherit the house and fortune."

"Something like that."

"What kind of mother says that to her son?"

"You already asked me that."

"What was your answer?"

"Shut up."

"That's what you should have said to your mother."

"She did shut up, without my having to tell her to."

"Is there a legally binding document, to ratify her request?"

Karl remembered his mother at, for some reason, the dining room table of the house he lived in and would own if he could stand to do what she'd stipulated, if indeed she'd stipulated it. And was not this Vetch correct in pointing out how unmotherly Belinda Floor's stipulation was? Could she really have made it, or was it the product of the derangement that followed the death of the person whom Karl—let's not choose words that veil the truth, however translucently—loved more than any other in the world? Mother Floor sat at the dining room table in the beautiful white peasant blouse with red embroidering. Also present, Karl Floor and Larchmont Jones; this memory was evidently of a time post–Karl's dead actual dad; post–the mother-son dinner dyad that Karl had found heavenly and Belinda lonely; post–the transient man-friends, some tolerable, some less so. Karl, then, was twelve or thirteen or fourteen or fifteen, the era of the white peasant blouse in question, a time when the boy was subject to rolling fun-house fits of rage, elation, and despair, the first and last not caused, perhaps, but intensified by the dark trinity of the newly composed family dinner table. And why must the man sit at the head? What was that about?

Why was a table that did not previously have a head made to have one by this new older male, who'd arrived into a perfectly accept-able two-person dinner ritual seemingly inseparable from his cra-vats, colognes, goatee, and monologues?

The dining room table had gold, clawed feet and was made of a fine, dark, quietly polished wood, had rounded ends and fitted pads to prevent spilled food and drink from bleeding through the linen cloth to the wood, "because wood comes from trees, as we all know, which, in order to stay alive, must absorb air, water, and nu-trients, and this very property of the wood that keeps it alive can make it ugly when it's dead," said the man who was then new to the house, Larchmont Jones, with a wink at Karl, one of the reper-tory of gestures during the long dinnertime disquisitions that caused Karl to want to tell the man to blow him, though that out-come would of course have ultimately been unacceptable. And there was the sideboard groaning with dinner foods, half of a duet of groans of boy and former tree. And what would cause a person to buy a little wooden stand whose purpose was to display a plate, eating surface facing out for diners to consider as they ate their food? Maybe it was the not-completely-despicable sentiment that *Isn't it amazing how sometimes ordinary household objects if looked at in the right way can be works of art?* but you couldn't really trust most people with a sentiment like that because experience had sug-gested to Karl that there wasn't a sturdy enough partition in the human heart between it and the one that went, *Isn't this plate cer-tain evidence of the perfect commingling in me of wealth and discernment?* In any case, the sideboard plate display was new to the boy and alien to the family culture he'd been naturalized into, as was the jackass who'd brought it.

But the point was, there sat his mother in her auxiliary spot at the dining room table in the mind of the son who'd survived her, listening inscrutably to the maniac, the cause of the trouble, discourse interminably on the troubles in the Golan Heights, the challenges that beset the American labor movement, the Women's National Basketball Association, oil drilling in the Arctic wilderness, or the economy, stupid—perfectly good subjects ruined by the man who held them captive in his mouth. And what was this lady doing in Karl's mind as he stood in this unlikely kitchen of his twenty-seventh year? There was, that he could tell, no incident on the night of the dinner now in his thoughts, if such a dinner had existed outside of them, no remark or action of his mother's for him to remember her by. This may just have been one of those quiet image-clusters passing through one's brain on its own time, a messageless emissary from the old world to the new, his ordinary mother in her crisp blouse come back through the revolving door of time.

Karl looked up at Sylvia Vetch, whose hand was on the top of his head. He was sitting on the grimy kitchen floor. "You done with your work break now?"

"Why am I sitting down?"

"I don't know, what about my question?"

"What question?"

"Is there a legally binding document?"

"Why do you insist on this?"

"Because it's controlling your life."

"Who are you?"

"Why do you keep asking me that?"

"Because I don't know who you are."

She helped him to his feet with her sweaty hand. "This is who I am." She stood and looked at him, inches from his body, taut, a violin string in pants, toes grimed along the seams, hair black, straight, pulled up in a bun. He was dizzy, and left the kitchen.

"Where you going?"

He vectored for the front door, out of it, back down into the dark backyard, cut off from the sun by trees. Out in the small plot of grass and sand and fragrant conifers with soft brown flaky bark, he had another memory of his mother, the one of her in a sunlit room at the hospice on white and sunshine-smelling sheets, bed cranked up, face immobilized, pale and waxy in a predeath mask. He started toward the woods he'd come up from, and in which he'd been held by the woman he'd just left standing in the house above him, but then, the hug in mind, went back up the hill along the side of the house and in the front door. Stony, his back to Karl, stood in the kitchen where Karl had stood, and Sylvia had not moved from her spot. Stony wore Karl's yellow hat. "I'm Karl," he said. "I got beat up by two boys. My mother is dead. One day I'm gonna own her house!" Sylvia laughed, saw Karl, stopped. Stony turned, saw Karl, snatched the hat from his head, turned back, hid his face from Karl. Sylvia did not. Hers was agonized. A soft cry escaped it. Karl fled.

FOUR

HE RETURNED HOME. There was no worse violation of a soul than hope. He showered in the bathroom with the lesser towels, "his" bathroom; the possession of bathrooms and the consistency of towels, were these the important considerations in the life of a young man? Meandering in the dark hallway he had met her in the day before, he heard badly played piano music. Larchmont Jones this fine Saturday afternoon in spring was home attempting Chopin's Nocturne No. 4 in F, Op. 15 No. 1. He worked the first theme repeatedly, like a high school marching band tromping back and forth on the balding patch of grass next to the faculty parking lot. The piano was in the rec room next to the pool table. Chords made their way doggedly up the stairs. He thought of his blended family's passions for the rec room's two adjacent items of furniture. He and this man had played a game of pool while his mother practiced this same song. The two immovable objects were close enough that for some shots a focused player might tap the lustrous black body of the Steinway baby grand with the butt of his cue. They had placed, man and boy, a wager of ten dollars on the game, which Karl even at that time had understood to be nothing for the man and everything for himself, a concrete iteration of the stakes in the ongoing matchups the man had a genius for drawing him

into and he a genius for losing—a daily dose of death that he re-
sisted justifying as practice for the final one awaiting him. Jones
had sunk two stripes on the break and another on each of his next
three shots, then missed one, strategically, it seemed, leaving his
stepson to ponder how an arrangement of colored resin balls on a
flat felt surface could be so precise a physical embodiment of the
moral experience of humiliation. Teen-Karl—a creature whose ill-
fitting skin man-Karl had botched the molting of—uttered one of
the wrong remarks he was famous for in his own mind, the kind
the person who says them doesn't quite hear till they're outside his
head and then is powerless but to rue: "I wish she wouldn't practice when we're trying to play."

"Interesting"—the boy marveled at his adversary's ability to fash-
ion weapons from ordinary household objects such as *interesting*—
"that we have arrived at a moment in history when these two
activities can compete head-to-head in the same room of a
modest family home. Had one an old-fashioned godlike view of
humanity, now correctly proved immodest and false by leftist his-
torians, one might be able to assign a clear hierarchy of value to all
the leisure activities a given family could pursue, and from this
vantage pocket billiards would be so far down the staircase, if
you will, from serious music in the European tradition that one
wouldn't think of pitting the two against each other in a battle
of wills, let alone arrive at the conclusion that pool should be
given precedence over Chopin. But in today's modern world, in
which ours is surely not the only suburban house where a pool
table and a piano sit side by side like a pair of hippopotami cool-
ing in the river of bourgeois culture, and in which most of what
goes by the name of *value* has been rightly shown to be a matter
decided not by Nature but by Agreement, one cannot simply as-

sume the superiority of great music over parlor sport, so as far as that goes I take your point." He was diabolical. "On the other hand, old-fashioned though this too may sound to your young ears, I do believe there are times when the men of a household must defer to the wishes of its lady, so I advance the idea that we wrap up our game quickly and leave your mother to practice her instrument." Whereupon Karl missed his shot, Jones made one and missed one, Karl made two then missed, and Jones handily won the game along with its ten-dollar prize. Belinda Floor, mute of mouth in the rec room as at the dinner table, made manifest the darkness of her son's heart through the enraged tangle of bass notes that began the nocturne's second theme. Or so the young man at the top of the stairs twelve years later—now—liked to think, but music and memory were kinds of information mostly unsusceptible to literal deciphering. The moods they evoked were a wordless form of knowing that could leave a person feeling stupider than before he'd been awash in them.

The same pained piano tones traveled the air of the house repeatedly and without apology, like a series of farts produced by an old sick dog whose smell's effect on others is the least of his worries. The sound threatened Karl's delicate numbness. With no place to go, he came down the stairs, went for the door, and heard the word "Chopin.

"He composed that nocturne one winter on Majorca, do you know Majorca? I could show you on the map, let's go to the rec room and I'll show you. Or if you have to go out now that's fine. A world map, think about it, a map of the world. The entirety of the planet color-coded on a big piece of paper, every inch of land parceled into nation-states, 'landscape plotted and pieced,' as the poet Gerard Manley Hopkins put it, who was just a boy when

Chopin died, and he died quite young, late thirties. He got sick as a dog on Majorca, off the east coast of Spain, the same latitude as Wilmington, approximately—cold, in other words, in the winter, and him holed up in a Carthusian monastery—the Carthusians, interesting sect, hermits living together in humble clusters—very poor heat retention in these monasteries and who knows why Chopin chooses this place seeing as he's famous across the continent, all the hotels booked I suppose. The great composer's deep, bronchial cough resounds off the monastery's stone walls and the island's doctors come one by one to see him. On Christmas day he wrote to a friend, 'The first doctor said I was going to die. The second said I was dying. The third said I was dead.' It's good to have a sense of humor in these situations, and a companion, which in Chopin's case was George Sand. This was not a homosexual relationship, George Sand was a lady writer who took the name of a man and sometimes dressed in men's clothing. She had two children, they came along. His great French piano was held up in customs so he was composing on a tin can by all reports. You're Chopin and you're on Majorca and you're composing your nocturnes and your scherzos while running a fever and coughing up blood into this piece-of-junk musical instrument with your cross-dressing girlfriend's two kids fighting over a doll at your feet, now that's what I call genius."

Larchmont Jones was thin but had lately begun to bloat. He leaned in the doorway between the living room and front hall of the house, with his gray goatee, French-cuffed yellow monogrammed dress shirt, pressed khakis, slip-proof loafers with decorative leather tassels, and tight yellow knee socks to help the circulation, to which the calf muscle, Jones had once informed him, was crucial, an ancillary pump, a second little heart on the lower floor of the establishment. Every day now people wearing dress shirts arrived in Karl's life to impede him. Jones looked tired. His face was gray and red. The darker skin beneath the eyes was gathered in loose bunches like dusty drapes resting on a carpeted floor. Thin, frameless spectacles held the puffed-out end of his nose. He was neither pleasant nor well. "Tell me what I'm doing wrong," he said.

"What?"

"On the Chopin. I'm, you know, going for supreme delicacy, but uh."

It might be worthwhile to mention at this time that just when Karl had cut short Stony's imitation of him, complete with hat, he'd begun to feel a new kind of energy—let's call it *energy*—in his limbs and head. "I feel different," he'd already said to himself several times on the drive home and in the shower, reprising a famous line from the *Buffy the Vampire Slayer* television program. "I'd say you're within a thousand kilometers at most of supreme delicacy," he said now to Jones.

The older man raised an eyebrow in acknowledgment of his housemate's wit. "Just a few minutes of close listening, with sarcasm, even, I'd certainly appreciate. How for example would you say I'm handling the rubato?"

"What's rubato?"

"It's short for *tempo rubato*, which in Italian literally means 'robbed time,' and it's when you play some little bits of the song slower and others faster than the sheet music literally tells you to. Chopin encouraged this to give a piece of music that romantic feel."

"Well so I'm guessing rubato doesn't mean you play each note as if it was from a different song than all the other notes are from."

"Now you see? That's exactly the kind of useful criticism—
again, sarcasm notwithstanding—"

"I gotta go."

"Humor an old man."

"Which one?"

"The one who may well be out of your hair in a matter of
months."

"Why, are you going somewhere?"

"Maybe. And this place you're going with such urgency is?"

He didn't like Jones's slightly opened mouth. It, like his raised
eyebrow, acknowledged something, who knew what? He may really only have wanted piano help on this occasion, he was nothing
if not sentimental and self-involved, and often appeared not to
know he'd practically raped Karl a thousand times with his unhappy wit, but it also needed to be taken into account that he
hadn't yet remarked on Karl's face, and that he'd been known to
keep a comment to himself and use the silence that replaced it as a
filament to tether Karl to him. But Karl felt filament-proof, inocu-
lated if you will that very afternoon against being duped or bested
for at least the rest of the day, and, mistaking pain for wisdom,
chose to abandon the exit and enter the rec room.

"Now if this rec room were somehow the foyer of the famous
Steinway Hall in New York City, which was the biggest music
venue in town till they built Carnegie Hall, what you'd see here
would be one of each of every piano they made, including an example or two of their custom models for elite clients, because
while the backbone of their branding scheme was the ubiquity of
the piano—you had a piano because you had one and you didn't
question having one because you didn't question having a table
and plates to eat off of—the, uh, donut hole if I may now switch

metaphors of the brand was the whiff of rarity, the whiff of difficulty, of aspiration, it's got to hurt you a little to have a piano or
you wouldn't really want it. Was it the black American author
James Baldwin who said that the failure of the American labor
movement could be attributed to the symbolic desire of every
worker for the boss's daughter's hand in marriage? Am I making
sense here or am I just rambling?" Jones said as he played a few in-
augural chords that were not all that different to Karl from getting
punched. "The Steinways were Germans, by the way. Still are,
they've got a plant in Frankfurt I believe or Hamburg, cities that
sound alike to us but probably have little to do with each other if
you're actually German. They've got to this day a bold business
plan that bespeaks genius."

Karl had never been comforted by the power of boldness or genius. He really did hope in spite of everything he knew about life
that the meek would inherit the earth, though he didn't see how
they could all share it and be any better off than they were now.

Jones played the first theme once through and Karl paced more
rapidly than he felt Chopin would have wanted him to on the far
side of the pool table, keeping it at all times between the music and
himself.

"All right so what should I do here?"

"Take some piano lessons."

"It's a fair point. I get so busy during the week—someone's got
to slay the dragons—so I'm lucky if I get an hour here and there
to practice, and then too I'm restless, easily distracted. I'd do better
if there weren't a pool table also in this room. If each one had its
own room I'd be good at both, but as it is I'm *not* good at both. I
pushed your mother to move to a bigger house, even after she got
sick, but it eventually doesn't feel right, someone's leaving this

world and you're trying to get them to move to a bigger house. Now I guess you and I are stuck here, locked in mortal embrace so to speak."

"What do you mean?"

He sat up straight on the piano bench in right profile and cut his right eye toward Karl. "Should I dare?"

"Dare what?"

"Play the second theme."

"You could be sodomized by the second theme."

Jones played what seemed to Karl a loud, fast, random group of notes with both hands.

He knew Jones kept a permanent record of every aggression and would repay each in triplicate with any of his own far more various and refined modes of attack, often long after the fact, perhaps posthumously. Karl didn't care. A beautiful not-caring was happening to Karl; he knew he wasn't in charge of it and didn't care about that either. Things were really and truly changing, whether for the better or the worse hardly mattered.

Jones brought his head in close to the piano and set about extracting its keys with tongs. Valuing speed over precision, he worked fast, broke off half a key, tossed it behind him, moved on. Karl minded this tremendously. What was he doing here? He was investigating the way in which he didn't mind it all that much, or didn't mind it enough, or, given the fatalistic passivity with which he greeted the fact of it in his life, minded it an unacceptably large amount and still did nothing.

Jones was on his umpteenth go at the furious middle of the song. Karl understood this song. It described a life, in three parts. Melancholy prevailed in part one, the protagonist limping along in waltz time beneath its onerous weight. In part two, forces of oppression outside him were met by forces of resistance within him, giving rise to a violent battle. Part three, though almost identical to part one, depicted not melancholy but calm acceptance, the satisfaction of having spent one's soul on a fight and discovering it still in one's possession, damaged perhaps but amplified as well. Or on the other hand maybe the return to the sad waltz in part three showed how sadness not only always defeats all struggles against it but erases them, carries on as if they hadn't happened, except in those dreamy moments when one contemplates a new struggle, whereupon the dim memory of the previous struggle and its irredeemable cost extinguishes the spirit of struggle, resigns the protagonist to preserving the very limited energy remaining to him for the purpose of continuing to limp along under the weight of the sadness until on a merciful day it crushes him.

Karl removed himself to the side of the room farthest from the piano, where the entertainment center was located. He ranged around in and among machine-smoothed and varnished black wooden shelves, the flat-screen TV, the receiver, CD player, MP3 dock, turntable, two enormous speakers, each with its woofer and subwoofer; he drifted past a great assortment of CDs, DVDs, and LPs; he wandered near those godless pews, the soft leather couch, love seat, and matching recliners on which were strewn the sacred texts, the TV guides and leisure sections of local and national newspapers.

Jones said, "Two hundred and ninety-eight laps around the couch is a mile, I've paced it off. A little exercise at your age wouldn't hurt, while you still can. I'm having trouble concentrating on the Chopin with you over there restlessly walking around. I thought you maybe were going to help but instead you're hindering. Shall we play a little bit of pool on a Saturday afternoon? I'm capitulating, in other words, to the desire to play pool. Philistinism wins another victory over art at 218 Dreyfus Road here in West Egg. Not that pool isn't a beautiful game with a rich history, and I don't in any way mean to underestimate the value of relaxation, a state which you sometimes simply cannot achieve, let's be realistic, while playing a Chopin nocturne. Relaxation especially for someone like you you'd think wouldn't be that hard. What do you have at stake in the world, after all? Whether some kid gets an A on a quiz on polynomial equations, if I'm using the correct term? No employees, no capital at risk, no equipment that amortizes while you sleep—and *amortize* means die, machines die, I've seen it happen, it's very sad, I've seen men weep, I've wept myself, the death of a machine the size of a blue whale, or, to be more accurate, the size of a series of four dozen giraffes' necks laid end to end and dropping dead, how many people can say they've witnessed that? Well, a lot, actually, but not in the suburbs of New York. The midwestern United States, yes. Detroit, yes, your Malaysian and Chinese manufacturing belts, yes, grown Malaysian men weeping by the side of a dead machine at which they have spent the whole of their lives laboring from age twelve on, the soul of a man in a sense given over to the machine, entrusted to the machine, which your man Karl Marx would call alienation, I have this idea that you are a Marxist based not on any theory of his I've ever heard you espouse but on your seeming refusal to make anything resembling money and on your occasional snide remark about the sort of work I do and the people I *exploit*, as you have called it, while with a clean conscience I use the term *employ*. Did you know the average annual wage of a Malaysian adult is the equivalent of fourteen thousand U.S. dollars? That means your typical worker there is earning above the U.S. minimum wage, which, in terms of Malaysian ringgits, is a lot of ringgits, it's possible to be comfortable in Kuala Lumpur and even more so in your outlying areas on far fewer than the forty-five or so thousand ringgits that fourteen thousand dollars is more or less the equivalent of— Malaysia, the sleeping giant, if you know what I mean, but back to my point, which is that of relaxation. I would kill to have your life. If I had your life I would devote my life to relaxation, I would be so good at pool I would be Jackie Gleason, I would be so good at pool I wouldn't care that I wasn't good at piano and was only a math teacher, not that I think some people shouldn't be math teachers, imagine the world without them, but the point is I can't have your life, a man of my particular talents and energies, if I had your life I would turn it back into my life in a matter of years, maybe months, some people in this world must make things while others must teach youngsters how to perform abstract operations, this fact was long ago established by minds far more sophisticated than yours, or even mine. But uh, any case, you, who are in biblical terms a lot more likely than I am to get into heaven, would enjoy it a lot more if you could learn to relax, speaking of which, how about a game of pool, aka pocket billiards, which would mean you'd have to get up, I don't know, maybe you're relaxed after all?"

Karl, not knowing what to do with the novel, excessive, worri-some amount of energy in his body, had at a certain point in his stepfather's discourse lain on his back on the pool table, having succeeded in removing all balls but one, which now impinged on a spot between his lower lumbar and sacral vertebrae, reproducing the sort of shooting pain in the left leg he'd have experienced had the disk between these two vertebrae herniated, as the event is called. The latter had happened to Jones, the result of his having sat for many years in a poorly constructed office chair at his job in the manufacturing sector.

"But technically, if you lying there on the pool table like, I don't know, a jellyfish is a form of rebellion, and I think it is, and I might add that it's about time, then I would say actually it's *not* a form of relaxation, and in fact as the orator and activist Martin Luther King Jr. amply demonstrated, nonviolent resistance is one of your least relaxing forms of disobedience. But in the case of Dr. King he had a legitimate gripe against a frighteningly powerful oppressor, whereas although I admit I am something of an asshole, I'm really not the oppressor I gather you think I am, I'm just an ir-repressible conversationalist, a man with a clinically diagnosed ex-cess of conviviality, trying to engage you via a couple pieces of interactive furniture here in the house we share. If I thought I'd have more luck with the wood shop I'd suggest we make a bird feeder together on this extremely pleasant spring afternoon, but I remember all too well—remember with a shudder, frankly—our last joint attempt at woodworking, and besides I just don't like ne-gotiating those basement stairs at this point in my life if I don't have to. So, in any case, you and I having reached on the Chopin it seems something of an impasse consisting of my bad playing and your high standards, I therefore ask you with all due solicitude if you'd like to join me in a friendly game of pool. All right, no re-sponse from you, probably my mistake for not putting my request in the interrogative. Karl, would you like to join me in a friendly game of pool?"

One of the by-products of the previous afternoon's beating be-ing sore and stiff muscles, Karl had begun a series of modest exper-iments in neck flexibility on the pool table's forgiving felt surface. He was in the process of slowly moving the oblong sphere of his noggin from side to side, letting first one bruised cheek and then the other come to rest on the felt. He viewed Larchmont Jones with the more open of his two eyes, the right one, and said, "I don't like playing pool with you."

"Why?"

"I don't like doing anything with you."

"And yet here we are, stuck with each other."

"Why do you keep saying that? What does it mean?"

"It means I think we should make the best of a difficult situation by playing pool, and then I'll take a nap if the pains associated with my disease will let me, and you can, I don't know, go have dinner with your friends, if such people exist."

"That was gratuitous."

"I meant only that I'd like to meet your companions because it does a man my age good to be stimulated by the presence of younger people but you don't ever bring them around, so I was, you know, lamenting that and it came out inappropriately, which I regret."

Karl slowly stood. He tried to think of what not playing pool with this man would entail. It would entail the quiet insanity of attempting to find something else with which to occupy his time during the remainder of the long afternoon, and time as of recently had become gelatinous, the seconds did not seem to want to flake off and die away one by one as was their custom, they clumped up before him, impeded forward movement, clogged his breathing holes—there were more and more of them, he was drowning in time. Leaving the house crossed his thoughts. The problem of leaving the house, though, now rivaled the problem of staying in the house, which was closely associated with the problem of the man with whom he shared it, which had confronted him most evenings and weekends for as long as he could remember, and which, feelingly, was not so very unlike being trapped in the man's stale, crumbed, salt-and-pepper beard, or salt-and-brown-shoe-polish, if one were aiming for visual accuracy. The problem of leaving the house, though, was that outside the house had that afternoon become one single enormous location, and he was certain—though he was too frightened to test his certainty empirically—that each part of this location would now resemble that pale face, the loveliest face he knew, made hideous two hours ago by a derision of which he was the object.

Karl stood up and, by not leaving the vicinity of the pool table, signaled his willingness to play. His life was an abomination. He broke and sank nothing, despaired. Billiards is torture. A soul can be dying, another exalting, and to the uninitiated watcher of a game of pool, this might look like a game of pool.

"I just, really, Malaysia, though, so much of me is tied up in it, and as you may well know, or perhaps not, I go there once a year, would love for you to accompany me next time, in the autumn, during your school's fall break. Fall break, there's a pair of nouns that once you reach a certain age you live in fear of them becoming verbs. Men break their hips in the shower too, it's less well documented than the hip breaks of the fairer sex, a virtual commonplace among your geriatric distaff set, all my lady peers either have one themselves or know someone who does."

"You're not that old."

"I can't believe I missed that shot. Your go. Serious about Malaysia though, what do you say? Anytime you feel like either answering my question or taking your pool shot would be fantastic."

Karl swayed in place, took his shot, missed.

"You scared to go to Malaysia?"

"No."

"You'll go then?"

"No."

"You're scared, I think you're scared. Nothing wrong with that, I'm scared too, that's why I'm asking you along. You can't sit next to me on the plane though, because I'm *very* scared of takeoffs and landings and I need to be seated next to a beautiful young woman at these times, the likelihood of which will be halved, or more, if you're sitting next to me. There's no guarantee that if you don't sit next to me I will definitely sit next to a beautiful young woman, but my luck in this area is almost impeccable, as is my luck with these people being excellent listeners, I don't know what it is, I just have a genius for getting very pretty young women to listen to me, I sort of angle my words right into their open and absorptive—is that a word, absorptive?—pores and they drink me right in. This is not in any way to be disrespectful or adulterous to your mom, I would never, but you're in the air, you're so terrified you think you're go-ing to crap your pants, the beautiful woman is there—she is always somehow there with her striped shirt—and you just cantilever the words into her waiting body and this is intoxicating, this is transcen-dental meditation on acid as we used to say in the early eighties. My point being you should come with me to Malaysia and face your fear, during fall break, not during fall break, this, the teaching of math, the passing on to the next generation of mathematical skills, it strikes me, should not matter as much as conquering your fears by coming with me to Malaysia matters. And fear by the way is gener-ally caused by ignorance, except when the thing you're afraid of is legitimately terrifying like a giant metal tub with wings that leaps up off the ground with two hundred people in it. But in your case, you don't know Malaysia, you're scared of Malaysia, this is a story as old as the Malay Peninsula itself."

"I'm not scared."

"What then?"

"I don't like you!"

"My response: you're scared. Let us begin—what's the word I'm looking for?—desensitization by looking at a map of Malaysia, oh! And there's the eight ball in the side pocket, we are done with that game, my friend, you rack them up, I'll roll down the map."

Karl did not rack them up. The face of his stepfather, Larchmont Jones, was ruddy and flushed. Karl was no physician and did not know if this was a sign of good or ill health. Jones did seem to have benefited from an influx of energy sometime in the twenty minutes since they'd met in the front hallway of the house. Was he young and energetic for his age or old and infirm for his age? What was his age? Karl wished, begged God for peace from thoughts. As Jones entered the brief passage of blank floor between the pool table and the entertainment center, Karl took the rat's-eye view of the room. By a black piano leg, from the bottom of the beige wainscoting, tiny mental Karl looked out at all he could see. He saw the distressed body of Karl, limned in angry electricity, that bruised, puffed, agonized face so astonishingly unsympathetic. He saw Jones in pressed leisurewear, stooped and ruddy, the fragile body incommensurate with the prodigious energy that ran through it whose provenance was a mystery to rat's-eye Karl and to the one of full stature.

The map was furled on the wall above Jones. He reached up the way old people reach up, their skeletons remade by time to reach only straight out or down without strain. From the top of the Tower of Pisa four hundred years before, Galileo Galilei had proved the earth's gravitational field acted equally on objects of unequal size. It had perhaps not occurred to the great astronomer to investigate how gravity acted on the young animal versus the old: this was where gravity revealed its inherent bias. Rat's-eye Karl, who was curious about the human species but did not participate in its cumbersome allegiances, detected on the face of real Karl a kind of impractical sympathy for the old man, a sadness on his behalf, a mourning for all those for whom reaching things a foot above their heads was onerous, which nonetheless did not neutralize his dislike of the man, ratcheted up now to hostility by events some of which were non-Jones-related. The map Jones pulled down with a groan startled Karl.

"Have you read the Koran?"

"Is this a quiz?"

"I'll take that as a no. Have you read the Bible? Cover to cover, I mean?"

"God."

"That's a fairly accurate one-word summary, yes, that's a succinctly delivered book report. How about the Bhagavad Gita? I'm just saying I find these to be important and interesting texts, I like to have them around for easy reference. The indigenous Malaysians are largely Muslim, and if you know anything about migration patterns throughout history it's not hard to imagine how that happened. I like in any case on my annual pilgrimage to Malaysia to stroll the factory floor and engage my subcontractors in a discussion of the finer points of Islamic law, known in Arabic as *sharia*, if I'm pronouncing that right, which means 'path to the well,' and is relevant for anyone doing business in that part of the world, since it presumably regulates aspects of life as diverse as banking and sex. There's an old joke about banking and sex that I won't tell right now since you'd have to know a fair amount about both to appreciate it. Now you look perturbed, that was not my intention. Here's this map, in any case. Now, where's Malaysia?"

This was a different map than the one that had hung from the wall of this room in his youth. This was a cruel kind of map with no names or national borders inscribed on it, just a six-foot-wide picture of the world flattened out and seen from above, with the top of one's head oriented northward, of course, and one's genitals, knees, and feet off to the south.

"The God's-eye view of the world," Jones went on—and rat's-eye Karl would have contested this, had he a voice—"but not if you don't know geography. Come on, you're an educator, you've got to know this. You don't know this? Do you really not know this?"

Karl wished Jones ill.

"Let's narrow it down, let's eliminate as many landmasses as we can that are not Malaysia. America you can presumably pick out. You know where Europe and Africa are. Can you point out all the places where Europe ends and Asia starts? China? Japan? Australia? India? Indonesia, for that matter? If you get Indonesia it's a hop, skip, and jump to getting Malaysia. I'm just, look, this is fun, isn't it? Geography is fun. Knowledge is fun and greater command of the facts might improve your self-esteem, you seem a little depressed lately, and by lately I mean since I met your mother a dozen years ago. This is humor, I say it deadpan but I mean it funny. Karl, buddy, hey."

The doorbell rang. The rec room's occupants looked at each other. Jones's eyebrows went up, quoting eyebrow raises in cinematic history. Jones often seemed to be quoting someone else's manner and phrases, Karl never knew whose.

Jones went for the door and Karl made use of the respite to lie down again on the pool table, all obstacles to comfort having been removed. There was a sweetness to Karl's experience of this piece

of furniture used in this way that was almost a corrective to the repeated mild suffering he'd endured via it across the vast desert of
his short life. Indeed, most of Karl's suffering was mild, but there
was so much of it that his two hundred mild sufferings a day were
the equivalent of another man's one horrifying suffering a day.

Again he explored the table's gentle felt surface with parts of
his head and face. And now in his relaxed state the brave thought
found its way to him through the thickets and brambles of his
melancholy: Sylvia Vetch had come back to beg his forgiveness
and renounce her friend Stony, and so the world beyond his house
would welcome him again.

An accidental convergence of architecture and décor in the
house Karl shared with his geographically knowledgeable stepfather let it be possible that a man lying on the pool table and
rolling his head around its surface could at a certain stage in this
free and easeful movement have an unimpeded view of the
house's front door and entrance hall, as Karl now did on that Saturday afternoon, and so he saw the older man place a small cluster of ten-dollar bills in the hand of each of the blond boys
who'd punched Karl in the face the day before, grab their shoulders, pivot them toward the door, and send them on their way.
Rat's-eye Karl, on the floorboards by the black piano leg, saw this
too, and took it far more philosophically than real Karl did.
Rat's-eye Karl liked it. Rat's-eye Karl, because of his intimate
connection with the sad man in whose stead he looked, sensed in
the breast of that man a new feeling developing. This was not the
new feeling the latter had been hoping for, the one born of his
bond of love and trust with the woman he'd wanted to believe
had come to rescue him from his life; that new good feeling was a
stillbirth, which he now cremated in the smithy of his soul. This

bad new feeling was much worse than the one it came in place of, but it would have to do.

Jones returned. Karl lay still. "It's not the intended use of the table. Could you at least let your feet dangle over the edge instead of putting your shoes on the felt? No? I'm sorry, the business with Malaysia, you're sore, but you'll feel better once you know where it is. Ignorance is painful and knowledge is consoling."

"Who was at the door?"

"Some young men I did some business with."

"Which young men?"

"Fellows from the high school, you may know them, Brent and, I can't remember the other's name, Tony, perhaps."

"I teach them trigonometry. What was your business with them?"

"Lawn mowing."

"What happened to the usual kid who mows the lawn, Matt, the nearsighted one who does such a bad job?"

"I misspoke. Not lawn mowing, hedge trimming, yard work, sort of thing."

"And for this you pay them each that much?"

"I pay them the going rate. Why the interrogation?"

Karl looked at Jones for signs of unease. There were some—his labored breath, blotchy red-gray skin, pearls of sweat beneath the hairline and nose—all present, however, before the transaction at the front door, and therefore not reliable indicators of whether Jones was a lying sack of shit.

"One more game of pool, and then we go our separate ways and each man confronts the challenges of his own life in solitude on this afternoon of our Lord."

Karl felt voltaic activity on the surface of his skin. He would demolish the old man in pool now, he would have to, or suffer immeasurably.

"Rack them up!" he said. It came out high and loud. He thought he saw Jones jump. He'd have liked to make him jump around the room like a panicked toad. He sensed that somewhere in this room on this afternoon was a boundary line that divided the past from the future, and, as with a boundary between one nation and another occurring in the middle of a swamp, the wanderer in time, as Karl surely was, might not sense when he'd crossed it. Aggression frightened him. Violence frightened him. Cruelty frightened him. He knew all men had the capacity to perpetrate them and felt the point of being a man was not to. More than humiliation or physical pain, it was the failure of the capacities of decency and restraint in the two boys who'd punched Karl that demoralized him; or, rather, the recognition of the fact of the weakness of those virtues in himself and their failure to prevail in that event over the baser forces in the boys. And now he knew the baser forces of the boys had merely been a stand-in for the baser forces of the man who'd just paid them, whose own body had become too weak a vessel for such forces—and what would come of Karl's own, this hour?

Karl stood, Jones racked. Karl broke, sank a stripe, sank a bank shot, a cut, a combination, then missed, a miss in which all the other misses of his life converged.

The room went dim. Karl found himself before the map. "That's Vietnam, my friend," the voice behind him said, "that your cue is touching. You're so close you may well taste Malaysia now. Unh!" That was Jones's groan of pleasure at having sunk a difficult shot. He sank another and then approached Karl brandishing, it seemed to Karl, his cue. "I'll need you to move to get a proper angle for this shot." Karl, with Malaysia in his thoughts, did not quite hear. "I just, all right, if that's, uh, okay, I think I've just—ooh." Karl felt something sharp in his side. He looked at the table in time to see a solid green ball disappear into a corner pocket. What just happened? Jones, on the pullback, had poked him hard in the kidney with the butt of his cue.

"You just poked me?"

"I asked you to get out of the way."

"I didn't hear you. Do you then just poke someone like that?"

"I didn't mean to," Jones said, and smiled as he'd done when he said, "Lawn mowing." "You picked a bad time to have discovered Malaysia."

The narrow end of Karl's cue broke on the bony part of Larchmont Jones's left shoulder; an eight- or ten-inch piece flew off, landed in the piano's guts, and sounded a faint chord. Jones dropped his cue and looked wide-eyed at Karl. Karl thought he saw him smile again, it was hard to say, since most of his attention went toward examining the damage to the cue. He let it drop to his side, holding it in his right hand about a foot from where it had broken off at the narrow end. He was choking up on the cue, one might say, and he lifted it and swung it at his stepfather's head. He had a tight grip but the impact hurt his hand all the same. He vowed to try to hit the head again without the pain this time. He hit it harder, in the same spot, and hurt his hand again. His hand was vibrating with pain, and sometimes a word will seem to emanate from the feature of the world it was presumably invented to refer to, and so the word *mushy*, to characterize the single bloody place on the left side of Larchmont Jones's skull that Karl had hit twice, arrived in Karl, and that—rather than the moment, a second later, when Jones's head hit the rec room floor—was when Karl knew he'd killed the man.

Karl dropped the cue and fled the house. Rat's-eye Karl sensed an opportunity in the supine Jones. He scurried toward the body, broke the skin on the nearest calf, and dug out a meal.

FIVE

HE WAS SURE he had explored his house and yard more thoroughly than most had explored theirs. On any number of days of not leaving his room, he took the opportunity of the self-imposed confinement to stand or sit or lie in every passage of that enclosure where his body would fit. He had stood, lonely as a bowling trophy, atop his dresser and surveyed the room from there as if looking down on an untrod valley populated with a host of wildflowers. He had reclined on his closet floor beneath piles of clothes and ancient broken toys and let himself, more than any man before or since, absorb by feel this singular location. At one of the exterior corners of his house, he had lain beneath the drainpipe in a rough storm and let his body be washed in the gushing rainwater's myriad and sometimes physically painful impurities. He had done, though, for reasons that didn't trouble him now, very little exploring of nearby towns and so was not immune to the pleasure of the unfamiliarity of the houses and trees and road signs and mailboxes and telephone poles that pirouetted past him out the window of the car this hot, fair weekend afternoon in his middle twenties on Long Island.

He had begun to work on a problem connected to the recent event that was not the problem of how the law would treat it and him. He knew there was no reason for him to run toward or away from the law when he was, as they say, soaking in it. Not just police, lawyers, and judges, but neighbors, co-workers, students, a barking dog, his car's tires, a blade of grass in the tread of his shoe, the broken cue on which his body's signature juices and whorls had left their trace: what was the deep homily of the hundred mercifully distracting police procedurals that could be enjoyed on his television set at any hour of the night or day if it wasn't that there was no thing living or otherwise that was not a potential agent or vessel of the law? The law was in each capillary of the world. He could spit out the window and his spit would be law. Were he launched into space in a transparent plexiglas egg, each cell in his body and every molecule of his surrogate womb would be law, the stars but law's blind eyes gazing at him with cold impartiality. No, law was not the problem that beset Karl's thoughts as he wandered the earth in his Volvo. He knew what the problem was but couldn't yet translate it into the language of thought.

Rising up before the hood of his car was not a town per se but an area of Centraldale zoned for commercial use. On his left and right were one-story shops with rectangular façades of plate glass. One of them was inevitably a place where American boys could put on white suits to learn to fight like boys from China and Japan. One was a place with people made of beige plastic in the window, looking serious and willful despite their festive Hawaiian shirts and bright beach hats. One had rows of magazines sun-faded to blueprint blue. One had doughnuts and crullers, one had dead fish on ice, one had money, one shoes, one tires, one would clean your clothes for you, one—whose clientele were mostly not from Centraldale—would darken your skin. The off-track betting shop had men out front smoking in their cheap lightweight jackets,

waiting for their long-shot horse to win, as Karl too had prover-
bially done for years. At the end of a row of shops was a business
that did not have a plate-glass window and whose regular head-
and-shoulder-size windows were dark, but which he knew
nonetheless to be open; he parked his car and went into it. He
paused inside the door and slowly let his optic nerves absorb what
little light there was, as if sitting in a darkened auditorium while
the lights gradually came up on act I of the local community the-
ater's production of *Othello*. The room was long and thin. The bar
was to his left and ran most of the length of the room. To his right
were a few small tables and a jukebox. The smell was of beer and
vague inoffensive BO, lightly lysoled. At the far end of the bar, a
beautiful woman swayed—not drunkenly. Foremost in his ear
were the badly played Chopin nocturne, the light soft click of billiard ball on billiard ball, the crack of the pool cue on the man's
shoulder, the one, two loud thumps of its butt on his head, and the
sack-of-potatoes sound, which took at least six seconds each time
he heard it, of the man crumpling to the floor, and so Karl did not
immediately understand that the cause or purpose of the woman's
graceful swaying was soft, slow music from the jukebox. Her back
was to him. She held a cigarette to what he assumed were her lips;
her shoulders came up and her ribs slightly up and out, the cigarette down to her side. A cloud of smoke came quickly down and
to her right, as could only have happened had she blown the
smoke out through her nose. He had not yet seen her face but no
one with an elegantly narrow torso, flared hips, long neck, and
easeful movements of the kind Karl now witnessed—and who had
exhaled smoke so commandingly through her nostrils—would
not also have had a beautiful face. She wore a white cowboy hat
and her dark hair was in a short ponytail. Her black untucked dress

shirt, seemingly sewn to match her body's size and form, was arrayed with tastefully small rhinestones that spelled out in cursive, from one shoulder blade to the other, MISS POPULAR HYBRID. From a narrow hallway at the back of the room emerged a tall, wide, big-handed man in old flannel who ought to have been named Rusty or Clem, except for the fact that he didn't have a mustache. Facing the woman and Karl but not, Karl thought, seeing the latter, he raised his right hand to the height of the woman's head as if preparing to slap her or perform semaphore. His left he placed around the woman's waist. He swayed with her. They jukebox slow-danced. Clem whispered something to her and she laughed, which gave Karl a momentary view of the top of the white cowboy hat.

The beating he had taken, the night of "partying," the lifetime of love and loss in the scant hours with Sylvia Vetch, and the murder's exertion had depleted Karl. He sat on a stool midway down and leaned on the bar for support as men do who've spent years of afternoons in bars. He saw Clem notice him and inform his lady of this with a nod of his head. He thought this establishment might now provide him with the unavoidable opportunity of another fight, he thought he might have two fights a day from now on and be dead at thirty, one less Volvo on the road. The beautiful woman disengaged herself from Clem and walked behind the bar. Clem went back into his narrow hall. She was, he knew now, the bartender, and Clem had merely let her know she had a client. Karl wondered how many of his misapprehensions of the world the world had the patience and resources to correct.

She approached him, her face an indistinct and mottled off-white moon floating on the black shirt that was not fully separate from the darkness of the bar.

"Karl," she said.

"Huh?"

"Look at me."

"What?"

"Look at me."

"Sylvia!"

"Karl, I'm—"

"Pour me a double."

"A double what?"

"What do you mean?"

"A double has to be a double *of* something."

"Really? I thought a double was a kind of drink, like a grass-hopper."

"It's not."

"What do people usually get doubles of?"

"Whiskey."

"That."

"Why?"

"Tough couple days."

She poured him it and winked and walked away. The wink was the worst. He downed the double to numb the wink and was drunk. She was no longer in the room. The jukebox was on its second or third slow song since he'd arrived.

She was gone a long time. Clem was gone. Karl was alone in the bar except for the sad woman who sang the song. Evidently all songs this machine played were of the same slowness and of a similar emotional tenor, a romanticized and belted-out sulk. This one, he thought, was called "Cry." She came back. She came along the bar at medium pace, eyes averted, not in shame, as he'd hoped, but in annoyance. As with faces, Karl was semiliterate in the language of bodies, but he squinted and tried and thought hers said she found him and his easily wounded and deterred affection a chore. Her face was blurred by his drink and the bar's dim light, whereas he remembered and had been made to swoon by the extra facial crispness of her. He didn't know if he could go on loving a woman with a blurry face. Each couple needed at least one person with sharp facial contours lest the two become a single fool.

"Dance with me," he said.

She tensed up. "I don't like to dance."

"You just did."

She pressed her lips together hard—two fat garden slugs making love—and still had not looked his way.

"At one time, in the forest, you wanted to hug me. One might also wish to believe you enjoyed it."

She exhaled in what Karl would normally have understood was exasperation, but something was off, he sensed he lacked at least one key piece of information whose absence prevented him from accurate assimilation of events now transpiring in this bar; this was not so dissimilar from the state of affairs of his days in general, with the difference that rather than staying still and keeping quiet as much as was possible, now he blundered on, acting and saying, damning the consequences even as, rough beasts, they slouched toward him to be borne.

She poured another double in his glass, retrieved a second glass of the same size from behind the bar, filled that one, raised it toward him, said, "To forgiveness," didn't mean it, downed her double, left glass and bottle on the bar, walked methodically around the bar, stood next to him, did not face him, still would not look him in the eye. "Well?" she said.

"What?"

"You gonna dance with me?"

"You gonna dance with *me*?"

"I'm here, ain't I?"

"You're supposed to face me."

She did. "Cry" was on again, or still. "Is this 'Cry'?" he asked.

"It's 'Wail,'" she said.

He put his arms around her and tried to sway with her but she would not. She glanced toward the back hall where Clem had gone. Karl put some muscle in his grip and pressed himself to her from knees to neck.

"Wait!" she said, and disengaged, and poured herself another double shot, and drank.

"You're in distress," it finally occurred to him to say. "Why?"

"I don't know."

"Yes you do."

"I mean, I know, but please don't ask me to talk about it now. Let's just dance."

"You don't seem to want to dance any more than you want to talk."

"I do. I like it."

"Really?"

She softened all at once and eased her hips into his.

He was strong now and controlled his body and thoughts and those of Sylvia, whom he danced, which she very much liked, deliberately up and down the dark and dirty bar floor to songs called "Sob," "Faint," "Come," and "Die." Because he knew her body's needs, he danced her toward the bar to take another double shot, and took one more himself; not much later, same again. A well-timed drink is like fifty dance lessons. A good dancer does not know what his partner wants, he teaches her what she wants, then does not give it to her, not all of it, not yet. Her mouth found his, in passing, and was soft and sophisticated, as he knew it would be, and careless yet considerate. They did not kiss so much as their mouths exchanged brief, pensive, tactile communications. He knew kung fu now too, and would use it on Clem if *that* eventuality arose. It did—it might. He—Clem—swam up through the back hall's gloom once more. She went stiff again, her skin repelled Karl's hands. Clem did not enter the room, he faded back into the hall, but Karl had lost the loving and submissive girl of the several dances. These changes astounded him. She'd already put the bar between them. She looked at him in fear, at the hall, the wall, the window, stools, bottles, jukebox, floor.

Her eyes found his. They were wet and further blurred. "What's happening? What happened?" she asked.

"I've killed Larchmont Jones."

"Larchmont Jones is my father!"

SIX

"HAVE YOU EVER TRIED being a man?" Karl asked. "It's difficult."

"Join the club."

"Which club?"

"The club of people for whom things are difficult."

"What are you doing back there?"

"Sobering up."

They were in his same old car again, he in front, driving, she in back, lying with her face in the torn and sandy seat. This was a piece-of-shit car, let it be said.

"You're making that hole bigger!"

"Watch the road! God, what a terrible week!"

"What?"

"I said it's been a hard week!"

"You brought it on yourself."

"I can't hear you."

"Come up here."

"I can't."

He stopped the car. They were on a road somewhere between one town and another, one of a thousand identical roads that were cracked on their sides, the cracks filled in with swamp grass and sand. A summer heat had come down. It buzzed in the brush nearby. He went around to the passenger side, yanked open the rusted back door, and grabbed a hand of hers that happened, in a series of random movements she was making to try to find a comfortable position on the seat, to have been stretched out above her head.

"What are you doing?"

"Pulling you out of the car."

"Get off."

"Get out of my car."

"You kicking me out of your car?"

"No, sit in the front, this is ridiculous."

"Man!" She crawled out and rested on her hands and knees amid the cracked asphalt and sand. "I am drunk off my ass."

"Why?"

"Can't tell you."

Having abandoned the car in the road, they stood on the lawn. The house loomed above them. He owned it now, according to the state, or his memory.

She cried and made an angry face. "You killed him."

"You lied."

"Killing's worse."

They went in. Larchmont Jones lay as if resting on the floor, a face-sized dark red pool beside and connected to his face. Karl stared down into the pool and saw his own face. Sylvia said, "Careful, you'll fall in love and get stuck to the floor."

He had never seen the man with eyes closed. The lids had fluttered at times when he searched for a word, and the fluttering had functioned then as a hand held out to stay speech, a *Shut up* uttered by the eyelids; what is a pool cue to the skull when compared with an adult male's effectively telling a child every day for years, *My life counts for more than yours?*

He was not resting. Karl's mother had been the nap-taker of the house, always on the living room couch. Her naps were both naps and performances of naps, giving her the rest she required and saying, *This is all very tiring*, leaving the men of the house to figure out what *this* and *all* might mean. Sleep could mean so much. One could sleep and be awake, like Karl, who did not know or thought he did not know how his mother had spent all her non-sleep time. The old man's open-mouthed gray-blue face looked pained. It would not, at least, he hoped, look *wry* again, but if you zoomed in on the dried lips and off-black hole of the mouth you could find yourself coming up against some difficult concepts.

Sylvia screamed. He eased her into the living room. He sat down on the couch on which his mom had napped, and into which he'd vomited a little yesterday after he'd met Sylvia. It smelled of disinfectant now; Jones had cleaned it with rolled-up sleeves before Karl killed him. She sat on the comfy chair across the coffee table from the couch, as before, five feet of dull domestic space between them. They looked at each other's eyes. Their eyes dug canals of looking in the air. The canals were fingers that touched.

"What do we do?"

"Bury him."

"No."

"Call the cops."

"No."

"Come here."

She came. She curled into his lap and they slept.

"Honeysuckle Rose" woke them up—tempo and ear feel, *sprightly*; piano style, *mediocre*.

She scrambled off of him and stood in the middle of the room, knees and elbows bent, torso straight and taut, neck a balanced pedestal for head. Sand clung to her black shirt and black jeans. She'd had black cowboy boots and had kicked them off somewhere, was sockless. Her feet gripped the Persian rug. Her skin gripped the air, or the music in the air. Her white cowboy hat was gone. "Every honeybee fills with jealousy when they see you out with me," which demoralized Karl. He had started liking having killed Jones. It had begun to give him a more resolute position from which to face the world—more Karlness to his Karl; it had also brought him back Sylvia. But now with "Honeysuckle Rose" the vagueness of being him had returned and he was stuck on the couch again and he wanted to kill Larchmont Jones again but he knew he'd missed his chance.

Night came down on Long Island. The windows went black. He said, "Do you think that's him playing?"

She looked at him with incredulity. The song stopped at ". . . you just have to touch my cup." She left, got as far as the dining room, came back. She dragged him off the couch and pushed him toward the rec room. They stopped at the dining room table, sat down, and put their heads in their hands. The house was quiet. They lifted up their heads. She jerked hers toward the rec room. Karl went in.

"Oh," Jones said, sitting on the piano stool, "it's you."

"Who were you expecting?"

"My daughter."

Karl pulled Sylvia, who was behind him, into the room.

"Hello, Sylvia."

"Hello, Monty."

"You can call me Dad."

"No, I can't."

His left eye, the one on the side of his head where his stepson had hit him, drooped. His cravat, which had been disheveled when he lay on the floor, was restored to order. He seemed his jaunty self, perhaps a shade pensive. "These jazz songs are really so enjoyable. They're not easier, necessarily, than the classic European pieces, but they provide levity. That nocturne seems to have depressed me. Come in, kids. Ignore the blurriness of the room. My children together in my house, I've long dreamt of this. Could you clean up in here while I go to bed?"

"Clean up?"

"Wipe the blood up off the floor and clean and dress the wound on the side of my head where you hit me with the fucking pool cue, yes."

He slumped over and would have fallen to the floor had she not caught him. She took his legs and Karl took his arms and they carried him up to his room, Sylvia shouting "Support his head!" on the stairs.

"Please," Karl said, when they'd cleaned his wound and bandaged him and tucked him into bed, "tell me we don't have the same mother."

"Murder you'll commit but incest is a bridge too far?"

"Yes!"

She took his hand in hers—her throwaway gestures left exhilaratingly little Karl in Karl—and said, "Come help me wash my shirt, it's got blood on it," and led him to the master bath.

He said, "This is *his* bathroom."

"I need the nicest possible bathroom right now."

She unbuttoned the Miss Popular Hybrid shirt, revealing a translucent indigo bra.

"What are you doing?"

"I told you, I need to wash my shirt. Fill the sink up with cold water."

"You're giving me orders now?"

"Does he have any laundry soap in here?"

"How should I know?"

"Look around!"

"Why should I?"

"Because you're helping me, bro, just like I helped you lug *him* up the stairs."

"Don't call me *bro*."

Karl bent down to look for detergent in the cabinet beneath the marble, scallop-shaped sink. It was really nice in this bathroom, he liked it in here now: pale blue walls, soft light that articulated objects clearly and flattered the face, and floating above him in their dark bra, Sylvia Vetch's breasts, which did not overstep the modesty of nature in their size, but, in shape, and buoyancy, outran even the great statuary with which he had occupied himself for a period in his youth.

"Is there any down there?"

"No, but look at these beautiful plumbing fixtures."

"Don't start adoring plumbing. My breasts, by the way, don't get dirtied or damaged by contact with your looking, you don't need to try to hide it, I like it."

He grew hot from hair to shoes. Because he had seen Peter Paul Rubens's painting of the blameless Susanna being looked at by the lascivious elders of her local synagogue, Karl knew what skin looked like that was loath to be looked at, and so he said, "You bluster."

"What?"

"You stand there inviting me to look at you in your bra but you've got like an anorak of toughness on over your real self to conceal it from view."

She opened her mouth but did not speak. Her arms fell to her sides. She turned her head away from him. He looked at the irregularly shaped dot of red on her high, pale cheek, just beneath her livid lower eyelid. He wanted to know everything about the world this square inch of skin could reveal to him.

"Go find the soap."

"Did you know I'd be in the house when you came here yesterday?"

"Yes."

"You knew of my existence."

"And you really, truly didn't know of mine?"

"No."

"That was my first shock with you the other day was your complete nonrecognition of me, your utter inability to figure out who I was, when I'd seen you from afar at least a dozen times."

"So you really grew up right over in Centraldale? Were you poor?"

"Not really, but my dad thought so. When he started making serious money, my mom and me were like the poverty he had to leave behind. I was the dingy old fridge and she was the dingy old oven in the dark little Centraldale house and we wouldn't look right in the new big Seacrest place so he got new ones—a nice new out-of-it middle-class wife and kid who were untainted by ever having had to struggle to keep it together."

"That's not a nice thing to say."

"He tried to keep the families a secret from each other—I didn't know he'd remarried till months after the wedding—but

I mean come on, how could you not know? I guess how psychologically damaged you are makes you a mental retard?"

"Probably."

"Stop pretending that being accommodating isn't just a form of aggression."

"Really? *You're* accusing someone of pretending something?"

"Go get the soap."

"What was your second shock?"

"What?"

"You said your first shock was that I didn't recognize you."

"Oh. My second shock was how genuinely innocent you are, not to say hapless. It's really pretty amazingly endearing and sweet. You're like the anti-Stony. Soap!"

He passed through the bedroom on his way to the hall, looked at the helpless old man asleep in his bed, saw that a pastel orange stain had grown on the bandage around the wound, was troubled by a presentiment, descended to the basement, was menaced there by large shapes, found the soap in the white bottle that had come to symbolize trustworthiness and inevitability, came back up the stairs, averted his gaze from the bed, found, by the bath, the thin, pale, muscled back of Sylvia and its blue horizontal bisector.

"Did you come here yesterday specifically to meet me?"

"Pour in the soap."

"Why did you conceal who you were?"

"I don't know, when I realized you didn't know who I was I decided I wanted to be this mysterious stranger you would fall in love with."

"That sounds highly implausible."

"Pour."

He did. The soap settled to the bottom of the sinkful of cold water.

"Now here," she said, placed her palm on the back of his hand, closed her fingers around it, and guided it into the water. "Swirl it around. See? This is how we wash a shirt by hand."

"Oh."

"Your shirt is bloodied too, it stinks of fear."

"What does fear smell like?"

"If you'd been around it as often as I have, you'd know."

The inchoate biography of hardship formed of such remarks was a waist-high, still-boneless homunculus wetly laboring for breath behind the plastic curtain on the bathtub floor.

"Throw it in," she said, referring, he assumed, to his shirt. She said it impatiently, as she'd said more than half the things he'd heard her say. Maybe she wasn't worth all this trouble. And though he didn't know what trouble he meant, he felt, in the bathroom of his wounded stepfather, like a groom at the altar who noticed, as she came toward him in time to a march composed by a German proto-fascist, that his bride's teeth, like those of her quarrelsome mother, were yellow and long.

"I think," she said, "that you think I harshly judge all you say and do. I don't. I'm in distress. I will tell you why but not now. Please accept that. And please know that I don't judge you except favorably, and so when you take off your shirt I will be inclined to like your chest because it's yours. I think you think I have perfectionistic standards. I don't. I have great curiosity and interest. It's just right now I'm kind of immensely challenged. Here, I'll take it off for you. Relax, it's all right, it's just shirt-washing, I promise, we'll go one button at a time, nice and slow. There. And now that one. And now that one."

He could see she made a careful effort not to touch his skin with her fingers any more than was absolutely required for the task. He felt by removing his shirt she was removing the blazonry that covered his mind and was looking directly at it. Buttons undone, she said, "Do you want me also to—"

He nodded.

She slipped the shirt, whose checks had been orange when new but now were brown, off his shoulders with, again, demonstrative care not to touch that which needn't have been touched. It dangled now from the two fingers she held up to him, playfully, he thought, as she stood there in, after all, her superwispy bra.

"Throw it in," she said again, not impatiently this time. "Now push it down beneath the surface and hold it there till the bubbles stop coming up, just as if you were drowning a sack of kittens in a river."

He held the shirts down, felt the little bubbles rise along his wrists, and used the mirror above the sink to watch Sylvia Vetch lower her gymnastic form onto the soft curve of the bathtub's rim. He watched her hand darken against its white. He watched her soft belly framed by the hard columns of her arms. Shirts satisfactorily submerged, he turned to face her, leaned back against the sink's rim, felt its wetness soak through his pants, was reminded of a similar wetness, probably comprised of spilled beer, that he'd felt the previous night at the house party whose key event he was sure lived on in a bubble in him his thoughts couldn't penetrate.

"So," she said, "here we are in my estranged father's bathroom."

Tones can be tough for everyone and were extratough for Karl, who was lately an avid pupil in the urgent remedial project of tones.

"You know you've got his blood on your face, too, right?" she said.

"Or mine."

"Your wounds have surely closed by now."

"My face has been jostled a lot recently."

"Let's wipe it up."

" 'Let's'?"

"I, *I'll* clean the blood off your face with a damp cloth, Karl."

This was the first time she'd uttered his name in his presence, and it had the effect of making him feel as if he existed.

To clean the blood from his face with the soft washcloth she'd found in the small shelved closet of the master bathroom, she needed to grip his right shoulder firmly with her left hand. It being too much for him to experience the calming pressure of her hand and the visual pleasure of her face at once, he turned his head away from her and caught, in a mirror of the same dimensions as many a television screen, a beautiful young doctor performing a minor medical task on the sad and scared face of her young male patient with the same intent focus she'd have given to a task of grave importance. He closed his eyes. She told him not to squeeze them shut so tight. She told him to relax his face and breathe. He did. Her slow dabs were so smooth, warm, and moist that he suspected she was making them with her tongue, but did not seek to verify.

The light touch on the edges of his wounds brought into his mind the thought about the wound of his stepdad that had been lurking at its periphery and he said, "We shouldn't have let him fall asleep."

"Why not?"

"People with head wounds aren't supposed to go to sleep, I think, right?"

"Well then let's wake him up."

"I'm already awake," Jones called from the next room.

They ran in, as if his being awake of his own accord was cause for fright.

"Speaking of which, my dear boy, I'm glad you're finally having your belated sexual awakening, but I wish you hadn't chosen to locate it in my bathroom."

They thought they ought to march him around in the fresh air, get the blood flowing to the brain, so they took him down to the front yard, each supporting an arm. The moon slept beneath the earth. The streetlamps had shut off but the sun was not yet up. The two young folks struggled with their weakened charge back and forth across the lawn with only the stars to light their way.

"A mouth even at the best of times is a place of turmoil on the body of a man of a certain age," he said. "Really for anyone the mouth presents a complicated set of problems. That Nazi bastard— who do I mean here, kids?—the mythographer, this is not a rhetorical question, some chatter from the dugout would be encouraging, unless you mean to bludgeon me again."

"Joseph Campbell," his daughter said.

"Good girl. 'Every living cell has a hungry mouth to feed,' or words to that effect. The mouth is the crude helpmeet to hunger. When it comes to feeding, let's face it, the hands are more intelligent than the mouth. The mouth also has to talk and give off other signals about its owner's mood like a smile or a frown, and let's face it, moods are confusing. Moods confuse the brain too but at least the brain has equipment made to handle complexity, but what does the mouth have? Lips, teeth, tongue, gums, a soft thin roof over its head. It has to cope with everything a brain has to but has few of the resources. It's directly below the fanciest organ in the body and how could it not feel bad about this? You know whose mouth is fortunate in this regard is squids. A squid is basically a mouth with a lot of legs to service it. You ask a professional sailor which group of fish he'd least want to end up in the middle of at feeding time and he will not say barracuda or shark, he will say squid. My point being does the word *bridgework* mean anything to people of your generation? Something's cracked in there. I'll tell you this, Junior: if you were swinging for the brain I think you missed. Well, you hit once and missed once, and the time you missed you got my mouth. If I'd been your real father I assure you you'd have had adequate batting practice from an early age. No good reason a middle-class adult American male who isn't physically handicapped should not have mastered a baseball swing. Nor need this skill be limited to males. My daughter here, uh . . ."

"Sylvia."

"Sylvia I did regularly take to the batting cage until her mother and I reached our impasse. Not that I think a person would swing a stick quite so hard at the head of someone with whom she shared genetic material, just that if she did she wouldn't have done it like a pansy. My slippers are wet. I see shadowy figures."

"Should we take him to the hospital?"

"No, I mean in that car over there."

Suspended by his arms from the shoulders of the boy and girl, he nodded toward a parked car they hadn't noticed. They stood still and wordlessly watched the car take form in the undimming light. Each glanced back at the house as if to calculate how quickly they could get to safety behind its forward wall, for there were as Jones had observed two man-shaped shadows in the car that was parked at the edge of the lawn without having seemed to arrive there.

The man on the driver's side opened the door, stood up out of his seat, was tall, closed the door softly behind him, walked toward them across the grass in the vein of the one who knows he will prevail in the encounter—who knows, indeed, that this will be an encounter in which someone will prevail and someone will be prevailed over. He was Sylvia's friend Stony.

"Guess you killed the wrong guy," she whispered to Karl, and time was not slow enough for his mind to translate this remark into its native tongue before Stony said, "I'm especially glad to see you, Karl, because I've been wanting to apologize for the hat incident."

"Do you have the hat?"

"No. Sorry not to have brought it."

Karl, not hopeless in the art of understanding how what was meant differed from what was said, knew he'd twice been apologized to by a man who would continue to demean him. And he introduced Stony to Jones on the suspicion that they already knew each other, but he could not confirm this because Stony's "Stony Stonington, pleased to make your acquaintance" was suffused with one of the ambiguous tones with which he seemed to suffuse everything, and because Jones's uncharacteristically passive response might have been caused by his head wound.

Stony said to Sylvia, "You sure change dance partners at lightning speed," another remark that was like the prow of a ship whose stern was not to arrive in the port of Karl for some time. Sylvia's noticeable tensing up was easy enough to explain as a reaction to being out of doors in her bra on a cool spring morning with three men in the emerging light, and I think we would be remiss if we did not commend Karl's earnest effort not to notice the effect of the coolness of the air on the *bra region* of Sylvia too eagerly on this occasion in the company of her father and her friend.

Larchmont Jones said, "I'd love to sit down now if I may be permitted."

"Are you all right?"

"No."

"Karl, take him inside."

Karl brought him to the downstairs bathroom and did the moral equivalent of holding back his hair while he kneeled before the toilet and completed a round of vomiting. When he had regained the power of speech, Jones asked Karl to please get out of the bathroom as quickly as his legs would carry him and essentially to leave him, Jones, the fuck alone for the duration of his life, an amount of time his estimation of which he'd just revised sharply downward thanks to Karl.

Karl stood at the southern edge of the living room, beyond the reach of its rug, and gazed out its picture window at his home's moat and doily, the front yard. Half the sun was up above the houses to the east. Sylvia marched erratically around the lawn, followed closely by Stony. She moved right, then left in an untucked blue dress shirt she must quickly have retrieved from the plentiful closet of Jones while Karl stood guard above his buckled form at the bowl. Stony's athleticism aided him in leaving little light between himself and her, behind whom pale blue shirttails billowed. His mouth moved, hers did, his did, and both at once. She stopped, turned, faced him on a flagstone, fists on hips. A fusillade of words from her to him. He laughed—silently for Karl. She slapped his face. He slapped hers. Karl was out the door and heading for Sylvia, Stony for his car. Karl reached her as his rival got in and drove away.

"Who *is* he?"

"Well, he's Stony Stonington."

"What just happened?"

"Guess who was in the car with him."

"Who?"

"Arv. Think about that."

"I will."

"And think about why two random boys from your school punched your face."

"I have been."

"And?"

"Not so random?"

"Right."

"Did it have to do with the guy who stole my hat?"

"Yes, genius."

"Why are you mad at me now?"

"I'm not mad at you."

"Yes you are."

"No I'm not!"

"Why would *he* have me beaten up?"

"Maybe because he knew I had a crush on you."

"You had a crush on me before you met me?"

"Yes."

"Why?"

"No reason I can think of now."

"Don't say that, that hurts."

"Sorry."

"Do you have a crush on me now?" Karl winced as if another punch were on its way, emanating, if you traced it back, from the same source as the previous ones.

"Yes."

"Why?"

"Don't know."

"Say one reason why."

"Because you're beautiful."

"I am deeply suspicious of that response."

"And you're sad. I trust sad boys more than mad boys."

"But I'm a mad boy too," he said, looking in the direction of the bedroom window of the man he'd hoped he'd killed.

"Guess I like mad boys too," she said, looking in the direction in which the handsome man had driven off in a car that Karl now retroactively noticed was elegant, expensive, white, and new, a Jaguar of some kind, he supposed.

SEVEN

KARL CLIMBED THE STAIRS to his brown-gray room to
log a few more hours of a life imprisonment that was no less severe for frequent furloughs of short duration. Sleep was for him as
for incarcerated men everywhere a way to speed along the hours,
and while his bed, that narrow plank against a smudged wall, testi-
fied to the grotesque insufficiency of this grown man's voluptuary
life, it was also the most streamlined equipment for the discipline
of slumber, no square inch not made use of: body down, good-
bye world, eyelids down; eyelids up, hello world, body up, good-bye
shitty bed for the next sixteen hours, or fourteen hours, or twelve
hours, or ten hours, or eight hours.

There was another strange woman in the house, in his room,
sitting on his windowsill, feet up on the seat of his hard wooden
desk chair, wearing a peasant blouse, as if one were not permitted
a change of clothes in the afterlife.

"Hi Karl."

"Hi."

"It's Belinda."

"Yes."

"Your mother."

"I know."

She laughed.

"Why you laughing?"

"You said, 'I know.'"

"I do know."

"You don't know anything." She laughed again.

"Hey!"

"Well, you know some things, but you act as if you don't."

"What do you mean?"

"What *do* I mean?"

"I've been trying hard to remember you."

"Trying hard, my ass."

"Mom!"

"Remember away." Palms up, fingertips pointed toward each other, she ran her hands down her sides and ended with a flourish out toward Karl, the body's way of saying about itself, *Here I am.* He looked at her dark hair, swarthy skin, bloodred toenails on the pale brown chair. He wondered if her hair and skin had been so dark in life, knew her smirk was her response to this silent thought.

"Do the math," she said.

"What math?"

"Are you not a professor of mathematics?"

"High school math teacher."

"All the more reason to sharpen your skills with an equation."

"What equation?"

"$2x \times 4y = 180$."

"What about it?"

"Solve it."

"It's stupid."

She started to climb out the window.

"All right, I'll solve it right now, out loud, to your face. I can't believe how basic this is. If x is one, y is ten. If x is two, y is twenty."

"Wow, unbelievable, not even close."

Karl began to sweat. "Wait, I meant . . . if x is two, y is five."

She shook her head. "Try using negative numbers."

"Why?"

"To correct a deficiency."

"What?"

"You don't notice what's not there."

"What do you mean?"

"I mean that for any person, at any time, what is not there constitutes an amount of stuff whose difference from one hundred percent of the world is statistically negligible, to express it numerically."

"All right, so, if x is one, y is *minus* ten?"

She laughed again.

"But I know I'm getting *one* of the numbers right."

"My dear, don't you know that to be half right is to be all wrong?"

"How can that be?"

"And yet it is."

She sat beside him on his narrow bed, softly stroked his cheek, and stared into his eyes. He stared back at her and cried.

He woke and went to the room of the man he'd thought he'd killed. There was residual annoyance about his being alive. He stood in the doorway and gazed at the oblong head resting on the high-thread-count pillowcase like a mutated fruit that would cause the one who bit it endless misery.

The fruit opened its eyes. "Let's go for a ride."

"You need to go to the emergency room?"

"No, somewhere else."

"Where?"

"You'll see."

"Are you going to retaliate for the beating?"

"No."

"Should I trust you?"

"Not up to me to figure out, numbnutz."

Karl tried to help his housemate down the stairs and out to the car and was elbowed in the ribs.

"Go to the Long Island Expressway and take a right, basically."

Karl drove. "We're going to the city?"

"Yes."

"What for?"

"You'll see."

"I'd like to know now."

"I don't have the energy to explain it to you."

"How much energy does it take?"

"With you, a lot. You're like one of those boys who has to live in a bubble of purified air to keep diseases away from his deficient immune system, only in your case the diseases are ordinary facts about the world, which apparently would kill you if you knew any."

Karl pulled the car over to the side of a street almost identical to his own, in front of a house hardly distinguishable from his. A Martian visiting this section of Long Island, unable to decipher signs designating street names, would be so confounded by the similarity of the streets, the two-story houses, and the bright, dense, mown lawns, that it would, as if trapped in the labyrinth of a sadistic god, die a little in its Martian soul; not a bad outcome from the human point of view: Martians drive down property values; their children are bullies and perform poorly on standard-ized tests.

"What are you doing?"

"Until you tell me where we're going, I'm not taking you there."

"Could it be the boy's testicles have belatedly descended?"

"It could."

They sat in the car without speaking and looked at the world in the windshield. Each man rolled down his window and took a gulp of air. In a tree nearby sang the ten thousandth robin of spring.

"You're taking me to visit my girlfriend."

"You have a girlfriend?"

"For about a year."

"How come you didn't tell me?"

"I figured the dozen and a half or so times I brought her to the house would be a sufficient clue."

"Where was I?"

"In your room. What do you do in there all that time, anyway?"

"I don't know." Karl started the car and pulled away from the curb. "And now you want me to meet her."

"I don't give a crap if you meet her. She and I have a date and I'm too under the weather to drive."

"A date, unbelievable."

"You're jealous."

"Of what?"

"That I have a girlfriend."

"No, it's the very concept of *girlfriend*, in the context of you, that confounds me."

"You have one too."

"What are you talking about?"

"She's your girlfriend." There were years when the monosyllable *she*, uttered by either to the other, meant only, and almost violently, Belinda Floor; two days had changed that.

"She's just someone who was in my house when I came home on Friday."

"Admittedly that sounds more like a wife. She's turned out quite wonderfully, despite her present difficulties."

"What are they?"

"I don't know, she won't tell me, but a father can sense when his daughter is upset."

"It really grosses me out that she's your daughter."

"You have my blessing, you know."

"For what?"

"To be her boyfriend, despite this other fellow who seems to be back in the picture and who, by the way, if you mess with him, you really ought to know what you're doing, which you don't."

"What is he to her?"

"Again, I don't know."

"I'm surprised I have your blessing."

"Why?"

"Because you hate me."

"Of course I hate you, you're an idiot and a schmuck and you tried to kill me."

They entered the Long Island Expressway, rolled up the windows, and drove west toward the city. They gazed at the road ahead, two suburban bumpkins on their way to the great metropolis. Buildings of increasing severity drifted past their eyes. At around Garden City—a place that had metastasized past the name Earth's first man had given it—fear entered the car through the vents; a

cubic foot of it lodged in each man's lungs. They trembled, tried
not to let each other see. Each fell back into his wounds, first ex-
aggerating, then undervaluing them, oscillating back and forth,
groping not for an accurate medical assessment but for the proper
moral one. How serious an affront to the integrity of each fellow's
noble soul had the attack on him been, and what was the appro-
priate response? The denizens of the Volvo's front seat tried first to
hate their attackers, then to forgive them, held each position im-
perfectly and briefly; so much hard discernment made them numb,
and so they remained till Queens.

"Here, here!" cried Jones. Consciousness reclaimed them from
their sabbath stupor and the car lurched onto the Brooklyn-Queens
Expressway.

"The BQE, Interstate Two Seven Eight," Jones said with the
professorial joviality Karl dreaded as a proctologist dreads a patient
on a bean-and-prune diet. The road's distinctive character evidently had begun to help Jones enlist it in a healing return to his
habitual activity of converting the world into a rambling mono-
logue. "In its heyday as a not-yet-actualized idea it really did eliminate congestion on your local streets and thoroughfares. One of its
proponents sold it to the citizens of Brooklyn by telling them they
could use it to get to the World's Fair in Flushing Meadows in less
than half the time it would otherwise have taken them. So it got
built, or partway built, and these Brooklyn men drove their wives
to the fair, and the wives wanted to experience the robot—the robot was a big hit with the ladies because they were invited to sit on
its lap and be groped by it—cold steel hands beneath skirts so long
and formless they doubled as family planning—how could an ordinary human male compete with that?—and thus were sown the
first seeds of resentment toward the BQE, except for the seeds of

resentment that were sown when hundreds of homes and shops were demolished to make way for it, and the other seeds of resentment that were sown when the thing ran right through the Red Hook section of Brooklyn in what is technically known, I swear to you, as an open-cut format, which means a canal is dug right through your neighborhood, the highway's laid down in it, and on summer nights the cars' poisonous exhaust fumes billow up out of the open cut, through the open window, and into the open lungs of your baby asleep in its crib, while in the meantime next door in your more affluent neighborhood of Brooklyn Heights a whole different BQE scenario is unfolding wherein the houses are untouched, no open cut is dug, onto the West Bank of Brooklyn Heights is grafted a thin strip of land where the westward-streaming road is stacked on top of its eastward-streaming brother, and on top of that is placed an eight-block-long wooden promenade on which the genteel and far more politically influential Heights residents—is there a location in the world with the word Heights in the title that is populated by your poor starving huddled masses yearning to be free? I would bet no—could stroll and sit on simple yet elegant benches and marvel at the man-made wonder of lower Manhattan across the East River with nary a car in sight, and I don't know if you've ever strolled on that particular promenade yourself but if you happen to be wearing a noseplug and earplugs and goggles and have thus sealed your major naturally formed head openings from the highway's smog, noise, and particulate matter, you can actually have a pleasant time, and only later do you note a taste in your mouth as if you'd just drunk a pint of Scotch aged for ten years in a hog trough. Another nice thing about the promenade is that if you were to happen to trip on a shoelace, don't worry, your fall would be broken by a toddler and/or shih tzu. Hey! Watch where you're going, Christ, did you not see that eighteen-wheeler? Remember the glory days when I taught you to drive at sixteen, an age from which you seem to have matured not a whit?" Karl hated him, hated him. "What a monstrous road though, to be fair to even your mediocre driving skills. You get a truck like that entering without an acceleration lane, that's an engraved invitation to a twenty-car pileup. Not to mention curves on this thing Jayne Mansfield, herself a traffic fatality, would be jealous of. And speaking of sex, your chief architect of this blighted artery was a gentleman by the name of Robert Moses, a slender, half-bald, rapacious little Jew who rammed his urban development projects down the city's throat, I truly admire the bastard, he reminds me of me except I'm nicer and therefore less successful— any case, Moses rented himself a suite atop the Marguerite Hotel, which overlooked his gestating BQE back in the day, and he had a phalanx of hookers on retainer in the anteroom to his office there, so whenever a crane lowered a section of the highway into place, he'd be staring down at it out the Marguerite penthouse's big picture window while coming to fruition in the backside of one of the young ladies, as if fucking the city itself. Exit here and make a left."

Brooklyn closed in around our boys. It hugged the car.

"Volvo. Volvo."

"Volvo."

"Volvo."

"Right at the light."

"What's the deal with the house?"

"You mean why have you continued to live in it when your roommate is abhorrent to you?"

"*Roommate*, Jesus."

"And will you own it when I die?"

"Yes."

"And what exactly did your mother stipulate about the house before she died?"

"How'd you know that's what I meant?"

"Brooklyn-induced telepathy."

"Your dickness knows no bottom."

"You'll never own the house."

"You said you wouldn't retaliate."

"That's not a retaliation, it's a fact. There's a parking spot."

"I hate parallel parking."

"Is that why you tried to kill me? To own the house? What a moron."

Karl parked angrily and walked around to open Jones's door. Behind, in a sense, the two-story vinyl-sided house they'd left on Long Island were ranged the set of twenty-story mud-gray residential towers they now walked toward on cracked concrete.

"Or maybe I'm the moron for telling you you'd get the house only if you were to live in it with me till my death, since I didn't anticipate you'd try to hasten the arrival of that event."

"You didn't tell me that, my mother did."

"No, she didn't. I told you she'd told it to me and asked me to pass it on to you, and I did so just after she died, when you were delirious with grief. That was underhanded of me, I admit now with little or no compunction."

Karl stopped on the short, poorly maintained path between the street and the closest of the ugly concrete towers that seemed designed to deprive the two men of the sun. On this late, mild Sunday afternoon in spring, isolated pairs and groups of kids walked and rode their bikes nearby, talking, shouting, laughing at jokes

Karl thought would make him wince if he could understand them, making all in all a hard sound whose purpose was to strike back against a place whose purpose was to thwart purpose, and whose name—the projects—had come to mean its own opposite. While trying to comprehend Jones's incomprehensible words, he looked around desperately for the sun. His hand, groping for a solid mass with which to steady him, landed on his companion's shoulder in a parody of affection.

"You're lying," Karl said.

"No. Then I was lying, now I'm not."

"Why did you lie?"

"I was delirious with grief too. I wanted you to stick around."

"Why?"

"Just because I'm not nice to you doesn't mean I'm not fond of you."

Jones moved them toward the tower's dirty plexiglas door as Karl attempted to parse Jones's trio of negations. A boy on a bike sprang into existence before Karl and bore down on him shouting, "Move out the way!" His last contact with a teen still vivid on his face, he stepped aside fast enough to receive the bike's wheels only with the toes on his left foot, a medium-intensity pressure he found almost pleasant. They arrived at the door.

"What are you stopping for?"

"Doesn't she have to buzz you in?"

"Yeah, right."

As they walked across a lobby not painted in years, nor mopped in months, nor swept in weeks—hygiene having abandoned its vigil against destitution—the questions Karl meant to ask about the house were shoved aside in his mind by questions to do with this other house of sorts and its occupant. Jones had found a way to assault his stepson's head that did not require a physical implement. Jones removed his phone from his pants, poked it, pressed it to his head, said, "We're in the elevator."

"I'll alert the press," said the woman in the phone.

He glanced at Karl and raised his eyebrows that were impatient when unraised.

They walked down a stale-bread-smelling hallway with peeling linoleum tiles. Jones knocked on a door. The woman who opened it was black, Karl noticed right away. She called Jones "Monty" and kissed him on the mouth. "Come on in," she said to Karl, "you can't catch it like a cold."

He felt her apartment was nice and as he tried to figure out why he also tried to notice things about his stepfather's girlfriend other than that she was black; this he did with mixed success as his noticing muscle after years of semi-atrophy had seen a lot of use this weekend.

"Henrietta Jones, Karl Floor."

"Now, Karl Floor, what are you having to drink? Because I'm going to serve it to you and sit with you and find out what possessed you to attack your father's head. Monty, the boy's not answering me. What do you suppose he's stunned by?"

"What isn't he stunned by?"

He gave his drink order and watched her move into the kitchen. His impression was of high energy and speed impeded by slow, pained flesh, surprised by the impediment though it was not new, annoyed by it, not resigned to it. Her feet, both of them, hurt, for which her strategy was to try to walk so quickly that neither would bear her weight against the hard kitchen floor for more than an instant, a strategy hindered by the slow movement of her legs, but aided by the light tan cushioned shoes. There were colors and shapes of ultracushioned late-middle-age shoe into whose mysteries Karl had not been initiated. The shoe was an item in the costuming scheme for a set of rituals designed to manage the bearable terror of bodily decline. That Henrietta's kitchen table supported a stack of magazines called *Prevention* confirmed this for Karl. He did not yet have to know about the shoes, the pills, the ointments and outpatient procedures of this period of his life, but when he did he'd be able to rely on *Prevention*, the monthly Leviticus of those Americans for whom retirement was no longer an abstract concept. The word chosen for the magazine's title, though, struck a note of hope belied by its own negativity, being the noun form of a verb whose implied object was *death*. No matter: this nice lady, despite the pain it caused her, was fixing him a coke. And here she came with it now on a tray, undergirded by the shoes. The color of the shoes, really, though found here and there in nature, was not found in the shoes of anyone under fifty. It was a few shades lighter than the current wearer's ankles; than, presumably, the feet inserted into them, than the arms and hands, the neck and face, though each of these parts was of a shade different from the others, making *black* a discordant word for anyone to whom actual skin color was relevant information. Her soft, short, kempt Afro, its tinge of red and streaks of white, her body shape and movement style, her mock-acerbic talk, her eye and mouth shape all suggested to Karl that a degree of goodwill was being extended him, a form of self-presentation deeply absent from "Monty," whose physical gestalt had given off practically the opposite vibe upon Karl's first meeting him and consistently thereafter.

Karl said, "So you wanted to know why I, uh, why I, uh—"

"Oh, forget it," she said.

Jones said, "Remember it."

"I'm not your confessor, for God's sake, just an interested party. Boys and their fathers are in a duel to the death the boy feels it's his birthright to win, and if he feels himself losing more often than not, he's liable to help nature along with sticks and stones. You're not the first. Should have done it about eight years ago though, when he could've hit back."

"Why are you both named Jones?" Karl felt sufficiently encouraged by her warm remarks to say.

The Joneses looked at each other as if their precocious three-year-old had asked how babies were made.

"Twenty-five years ago, Henrietta was my wife for a dozen or so years."

Karl silently tested the ramifications of this news while gazing idly at the forearms of the two older grownups as reflected in the pale brown tabletop whose high shine he associated with underclass striving.

"Why do you live here?"

"What do you mean?"

"What happened to you that you ended up in this godforsaken place?"

"If God forsook it, it's in good company," she said. "You done with your soda?"

"No."

She removed it from his hand and brought it to the kitchen with that efficiency of movement pain had taught her. From a kitchen egress Karl couldn't see, she vanished into a part of her home undreamt of in his philosophy.

"She can't hear you now so go ahead and say it out loud."

"Say what?"

"That my girlfriend is a mulattess." Jones settled back into the

worn vinyl dining chair with an air of accomplishment Karl recognized from those moments in his youth when this man had announced he'd won ten thousand dollars betting on the New York
Knicks, though now the somewhat stiffer body looked as if under
contract to give a performance it did not fully believe in.

Henrietta returned in a pale yellow button-down sweater beneath a bright red spring-weight coat. But to call the coat bright
red was not adequate. It had something in it—blue, maybe—that
stained the retina. Nearly everything and everyone had something
in it or them that you didn't notice at first, and if you did eventually notice it you semiconsciously elided or erased the noticing because you needed to conserve your limited energy even though
you were beginning to suspect that the erasure cost you more energy than the noticing would have, and the accumulation of era-
sures made its own hungry mouth to feed, and this added burden
made you feel fifty when you were twenty-six, and not a robust
and productive fifty but a worn-out, diminished one, as in that guy
in that poem who's just lying there in a hammock on someone
else's farm and sees a butterfly and smells some horse shit and hears
a cow moo far off in the distance and then he tells you he's wasted
his life all the while freeloading off someone else's hard work.

"Well, so," she said, "we have met, and will meet again, and now
it is time to begin my date with your step-pop, so grab your coat,
get your hat, remove your worries from my doorstep, and direct
your feet to your Volvo."

"Actually, someone took my hat and hasn't given it back."

"Was that person Charles Stonington?" she said.

"How did you know?"

"He's of the hat-taking kind."

The three were now bathed in the jaundiced hallway light.

"How do you know him?"

"He's done some business with my boyfriend and is a friend of our daughter."

"Sylvia?"

"The same."

"Then why is she white?"

"Oh, Monty, did he really just say that?"

"At least he's talking instead of hitting."

"Son, though I feel little good can come of knowing, I must ask why you are making a face as if a boa constrictor ate your poodle," she said.

"Because this hallway smells bad, and look at that paint peeling off the ceiling, I bet it's lead-based."

"So don't eat it."

"It's depressing here," Karl said.

"Why does he act like he's never seen a ghetto before?"

"Maybe he hasn't."

"I wish I couldn't remember the last time hanging around white people meant feeling like an education instead of a person."

Silently but with, it seemed to Karl, a wild energy beating back and forth among their bodies like a trapped bird, they rode down to the earth in the elevator's round-the-clock fluorescent gloom, and walked out into Brooklyn. The sunshine had all but drained from the sky and left a pink-brown residue of urban light. They walked toward Karl's car on the path between and beneath Hart Crane Towers.

"But you have to admit," Karl said, not knowing what compelled him, "that when you plunk down all these big, ugly, twenty-story slabs next to each other like this you create dark spaces no one wants to be in and everyone rushes through in fear for their lives, except the miscreants who want to rob them, or worse. There's no organic reason for people to be out and about in these dead zones between the buildings. If the city had thought to put the buildings next to the street, with retail shops on the first floor, then they would have created a natural social space everyone could move through without fear of mayhem."

"I find your thoughts on urban planning not without merit, but your math is a little off," she said.

"What math?"

"The part where you counted up to twenty."

Karl counted, blushed, said, "Twelve."

"Do you not, moreover," she said, "spend much time around grown-ups?"

"Why?"

"You act like someone who doesn't converse much. You blurt."

"My social skills are not very good."

"Come around again in a while and we'll practice. I'll leave you two to say farewell."

She eased herself back up the path. The boy who had ridden not quite unpleasantly over Karl's toes passed Henrietta, said, "You look like a flower today, Miss J.," and rode off. She sat down on a bench. Karl looked at her profile, was exhilarated by the mystery of another human being, and then was sort of lightly crushed by it.

He turned to Larchmont Jones and said, "Is Sylvia black?"

"Depends what you mean by black."

"Am I black?"

"Probably not."

He drove home, that long, pocked, near accident, the BQE, a blur.

At last he came that night, the end of the longest weekend of his life, back to his solitary cell. He looked at the sad, mottled brown of his faux wood walls and wondered who had chosen them and why. What good could come of such a choice? Did anyone in the world feel that this was the best, or second best, or third best of all wall coverings? Karl doubted it, and yet here it was, this décor abortion, flush against a million walls across the land. How many man-hours had been spent, how many contractors and day laborers had come into how many homes with their tape measures and their circular saws? How many fingers had been lost in the cutting of this grim stuff to fit snugly between the ceilings and floors of rumpus rooms and hapless boys' lairs? In what factories had it been made, in what nations of the world? How many men, women, and children had used up years of their lives at ten hours and one dollar a day in the service of people with so little imagination? How many dinosaurs had died to give the precious contents of their noble bodies to all the humans who could have done anything to their walls but chose to do this? The mass of men are hobgoblins of desperate conformity, wrote the great American poet Waldo Whiteman. Karl liked being solidly in the conformist camp, it gave him a place in the world, lent a sheen of dignified restraint to his daily hobgoblin behavior. He loved his faux wood walls. He turned on all the lights and watched them. He memorized each mark, line, ridge, and false wood-grain pattern some unremembered Audubon had painstakingly drawn while staring at the whorls the years had made in the flesh of a cut tree. Karl pressed his sad and damaged face against the gorgeous artistry. He paced around. He looked at all his posters. He loved his Hendrix and his Springsteen, his Klimt, his Klee, his Hulk, his Matisse and Van Gogh and his three Belgians, Brel, Magritte, and Van Damme.

There was enough visual richness here for a lifetime of looking. Inevitably, he found the only object in the room more surreal than a painting of a giant green apple in front of a man's head, and that was his own head, as seen by him in the mirror. How unlikely that this bruise-green and pink-faint straw-covered irregular surface, wrapped around an oblong spheroid form, after millennia, should have arrived at this place at this time.

He rattled down the hallway, brushed teeth he'd soon lose, rattled back, extinguished the lights, went to the window, looked at the yard purposelessly lit by the moon. A nightingale, upon a branch of his bedroom window's maple tree, as Karl eased into bed, sang to the moon in full voice what was probably in the bird world a lay of love, which filled Karl's heart with sorrow. He listened to it long and well till sleep, that burglar of consciousness, carried off the beautiful sound. And then an eagle, feathered black as tar, flew in through his window, landed on his chest, sank her long claws down past his ribs, tore out his heart, tore out her own heart from her own chest with her other set of claws, and replaced his heart with her bloody little bird one, all of which scared him more than any other thing he had ever experienced, and hurt like hell, whereupon she flew out his window and up toward the moon, still in the process of stuffing Karl's outsized human heart into her black little bird chest with her claws, or paws, or whatever those appendages were called on birds.

EIGHT

EMPTY HOUSE, WHITE CEREAL BOWL, banana flown in from southern parts, late spring sunshine on the breakfast nook, vague sounds in the street beyond the front wall: Monday morning, halting the weekender's free fall through time.

Karl was tired. Walking to school on the tan, granular sidewalk laid down by his municipality, he greeted the sight of the two blond boys coming toward him once again with an inchoate bring-it-on—not the I'd-adore-the-chance-to-kick-your-ass bring-it-on of his nation's current stepdad, but more in the vein of the more the merrier, his little eagle heart preparing him for death, or even life. They met abreast of the grave of his town's famous martyred tree, a stone elegy for a European plant that couldn't tough it out for the long haul in the New World.

"Good morning, Mr. Floor," they said.

Many a seventeen-year-old boy on Long Island in the era of our story had taken pains to limit the number of his facial expressions to five, lest his face assume a shape that corresponded to an un-preapproved feeling that would threaten the coherency of the young man he strove to believe he was. Karl admired the asceticism of making one's face assume only five shapes, like that of an artist who painted only seascapes, and only in beige, but the formal restriction not only did not help him decipher the content, it further obfuscated it for him, and so he muddled down the street unknowing.

They flanked him. All three walked toward school. "You don't have to talk to us if you don't want to, Mr. Floor," one of them said. They seemed mild now, and he wondered if their mildness would culminate in a second beat-down. His face could take the punching but his soul abhorred the waiting. The strength not to ask them if they'd hurt him must have come from the black bird heart in his breast; he hoped that it would last him all his days, and wondered how the bird would fare with his.

So he drifted down the sidewalk in a gauze of uncompleted thoughts, and through the hours and days of work and rest and all the movements of the self through time and space that were neither work nor rest. Larchmont Jones returned home by train. Weeks passed; no Vetch; why not? Vetch, for one, no doubt, and, for two, Karl. He could have found the house whose kitchen he'd been helping her to clean until he'd run from it and her and then run back to both to have the awful moment of the hat; but there were only so many roads Karl could make his thoughts travel on, and he could not make them go down the one called *look for her*. Weeks passed; no Vetch; but, at a certain point, Stony Stonington.

"Hi Karl."

"You took my hat."

"Yes."

"Give it back."

"I will."

"What do you want?"

"Oh, well, so much, don't you?"

Karl did, but didn't want to have that in common with Stony

because Stony was dreadful. And since today was the last day of school, and when Stony found him just now Karl had been walking out the glass-and-steel door of that venerable brick building that he wouldn't return to for at least two months, and had been acutely dreading the summer that awaited him beyond the door, a terrible transposition happened where for a second or more Stony *was* summer, and Karl suspected he wasn't the first person to mistake this man for a season.

He'd cleared the building and was out in the open now on the concrete by the flagpole, no safe objects in sight. Stony was in front of him and saying something he couldn't make sense of. The surgery-sharp ambiguity of the behavior at the back of trig of the boys who had punched him once so long ago, as sources of dread go, was as a thimbleful compared with this man and the impending season he stood in for or was.

"May I give you a lift?" Karl finally understood him to be saying.

"No thanks, I prefer to walk on such a beautiful day."

Like the day he'd been punched, today really was an objectively beautiful day, though its beauty was quite different in kind from that of the other one. That one had featured light-tan-spring-weight-shell weather whereas today fairly demanded the pale blue checked short-sleeve button-down shirt. The air was hotter, the leaves—hardly leaves back then—now moist and verdant, the flowers mashed up in big messes of vivid color, the trees aching with sap. That Stony would stonify all this Karl's heart rebelled against but was also largely paralyzed by.

"Mind if I walk with you then?"

"Yes."

"But it's a free country, right?"

"Maybe for you."

"Have I done something to displease you?"

"You took my hat and mocked me."

"Anything else?"

"Probably."

"I mock everyone."

"Great."

"We got off on the wrong foot with the hat."

"So give it back."

"I keep forgetting to bring it."

"I know what else."

"What?"

"You ruined summer."

"How?"

"By becoming it."

"Maybe, but I'd like to get to know you."

"Why?"

"Because you're someone new and significant in Sylvia's life and I've known her a long time and care about her."

"Haven't you known Larchmont Jones a long time too?"

"Yes, but I don't care about him. Just kidding," he said, and laughed to prove it.

With difficulty, Karl looked while walking, listening, and responding. The tailor who had made Stony's light blue shirt must have worked in collaboration with the deity who had made his long neck, chest, back, arms, face, and wavy chestnut hair. As for Stony's *being summer*, an assertion that, Karl noted, he did not contradict, the one who had made him may also have made the sun, air, and trees. By contrast, a weary and alienated Chinese teen had let herself be subsumed by an unfeeling shirt machine in the making of Karl's blue shirt—and to say *blue* for both men's shirts was to suggest that the sky and the surface of an oily puddle that reflected the sky were the same color. And Karl himself had been made not by Stony's exalted god but by one who had misbehaved and whose punishment was to be required to use second-rate materials and formulas whose result, also factoring in the disgruntlement of the maker, was Karl and people of his ilk, because he'd long ago figured out that the explanation for humanity was not a single all-knowing, all-powerful god but a cadre of man-making gods of different ranks and abilities, and that this business of all men being created equal was, while a noble sentiment, the equivalent in mathematics of saying that all the numbers from one to a billion were equal, i.e., bullshit.

Trees, cars, street signs, other people's heads rose up and fell away as he kept pace with Stony down the sidewalk toward his home. If this was Karl's walk, how had Stony come to set the pace for it?

". . . and so just as she was violating the sacrament of her marriage to my father, she started taking me to services at Francis Xavier in Seacrest, since that's where her new beau was to be found. And that's where I first laid eyes on Sylvia, who I know I don't have to tell you was just an electric thirteen-year-old in her white confirmation dress, I mean that girl was wired for sound and light, and though as a seventeen-year-old I should have been concentrating on older women with more flesh on their bones in terms of whom to find alone in a doorway somewhere, I just couldn't stop looking at Sylvia. So insolent, so trivial, so capricious, so mercenary, so careless, so hard to touch, so hard to turn—and yet so pretty!"

They'd come abreast of the little flat stone that always told the same story, the one about the elm tree whose place in the earth it had taken, a heroic tree by the stone's account, that fought valiantly and alone long after, it must have known, its kind had a future in the land. Had his unwanted companion on this final walk home from school of the year let him stop and contemplate the valiant and vanquished tree in silence as the little stone urged passersby to do, he might have isolated the single thought in his crowded mind that was making him so sad, but instead they walked on down the last stretch of sidewalk to his house, the thought lying in the grass somewhere near the stone.

". . . being loved back by her was quite simply the most profound and wonderful experience of my life. If I'd known that doing a little bit of business with her father once I got my M.B.A. would drive her away from me I'd never have done it. So when she came back to me four months ago and told me she loved me, who was I to say I didn't really sense that same passion from her as before? Anyway, as you can see, this has been a long time coming, and I'd like you to be there to witness it, because you're in the mix now, for reasons some of which are obvious to me. The dancing in the bar I wasn't initially too keen on, but let's face it, you're not much of a threat."

"What dancing?"

"In the bar."

"What bar?"

"My bar, in Centraldale, in April, the day after the party in the house I rent to her and her friends, where we met."

"That was you in that bar?"

"Yes."

"I thought that was Clem."

"Who's Clem?"

"The guy in that bar that day."

"That was me."

"You own it?"

"Yes."

"And her house?"

"Yes."

They'd arrived at the row of flagstones that led to Karl's house and bisected its lawn. And perhaps because they had just been speaking of houses, and ownership, they looked at the house and did not speak. Karl's latest sadness went out now to the house, attached itself to the black shutters, sash windows, gray vinyl siding, and found embedded there many previous of his sadnesses, and some belonging to Larchmont Jones, among all of which his own sadness felt, of course, at home.

"This is your stop," Stony said, and Karl turned himself from the house to Stony's face, where Stony's eyes had been waiting for him, floodlights blazing through the unprotected windows, exposing the clutter of the rooms. "So can I count on you?"

"For what?"

"To be there."

"Where?"

"Krüog Town Hall. I wanted it to be Francis Xavier but Sylvia insisted on a civil ceremony, ironically."

"What are you talking about?"

"What I've been talking about for the last fifteen minutes."

"Which is?"

"Wow, some witness you'll make."

"Of what?"

"Our wedding!"

His afternoon's brief cohort retreated from him while the blight of that man's news did not.

Now that it was too late, he went in search of her. He drove by feel, as Helen Keller had done for years in jokes. He found, miraculously, the gas station he'd once been driven to in this very Volvo by Arv. Luckily, he needed gas. The price of it was high for him, as was the price of everything. He got out of the car and thought he saw, through the glass, at the cash register, the one called Jen, who was in that group that probably knew more about his having wigged out at the party than he himself did, a group he imagined carrying his blacked-out self to the beach on their shoulders in the dark of night because Stony, successfully disguising his malevolence as youthful mischief, had told them to, "And I'll take his hat!" Not that Karl was a reliable arbiter of morality, but it worried him how, in groups like this and far larger than this, the logic of charisma—the sheer Stoniness of an individual, if you will—could be a substitute for reasoned ethical standards of behavior. He dipped his credit card in the gas pump's card-dipping area. It read his card and knew things about him even Jen didn't know. He pumped and was a vortex of products from afar: gas from Saudi Arabia, car from Sweden, shirt from China, card from Cardonia. He did not go to Jen for she would have confused him. He got in his car and circumnavigated the woods through which he'd once taken a shortcut from the gas station to Sylvia's house and there been hugged by her. The memory of the hug sent a shiver through his beleaguered body from north to south.

He recognized the blades of swamp grass on the road near the house, though they were older now, or were the children of the blades he'd seen two months ago. He eased the Volvo up the pebbled drive beneath the undescended drawbridge of thick summer tree branches. There was that one gray tree that was still leaning and dying. Sorry, tree. Here came Arv on foot with the forward-leaning Arv gait that made him an inadvertent figure of fun. Sorry, Arv. Arv signaled Karl to roll down his window though it was already down. He wondered if Arv would at some point turn vicious as comedic men sometimes do.

"She's a nasty piece of business and strong, too—bites, literally. Save yourself and leave her to Stony, he's the only one who can handle her," Arv said, leaning in toward Karl in his car. A plume of ancient halitosis issued from his mouth and enveloped Karl's head, physically connecting the two men. Arv told Karl he had to go, and went, and Karl drove on. Arv's remark and the sound each pebble made grinding against its brothers beneath the Volvo wheels and all the trees that lined the drive and everything that had happened in his life till now formed a prelude to the impending encounter.

She stood as if awaiting him, arms crossed, on the wide modernist front porch with no rails. The summer sun made her black hair shine, and made her pale face and pale, thin, strong arms glow. He had to remind himself she was black. He hadn't seen her since he'd heard the news, or, of course, that other news. Her ankles were thicker than before. Maybe she was turning into Henrietta Jones as daughters are said to do and would soon be fully black, completing a transformation she'd already begun in his head.

They did not speak, she did not unfold her arms. They walked toward each other and met in the transitional space that was neither lawn nor driveway but contained elements of both. They did not touch. He stared at her in sorrow and amazement and tried to figure out what she was staring at him in—not happiness, not relaxation. She turned and walked down the hill at the side of the house and into the backyard. He followed her. She went briskly, arms folded, through the backyard and into the woods behind it, eyes front all the while. If the movements of her body had been a form of communication they'd have been a business memo calling for an emergency meeting. Staff must arrive together but have the feeling of being alone. Agenda: urgent yet uncertain. She stopped at more or less the spot she'd hugged him on, a power spot for her, he guessed. She turned and looked at him again. Her arms were crossed in the manner of a clamp on her restless middle. He wanted her to hug him now but knew it was hopeless. They were two people facing one another in a small wooded area with an insurmountable distance between them. Her eyes yelled.

"Say it," she said.

"Don't talk so loud, I'm right next to you."

"Say it."

"You're marrying him."

"Now ask your questions."

"Why are you marrying him?"

"Why shouldn't I?"

"Do you want to?"

"Of course!"

"No you don't."

"Shut up."

"Really? We're at the *shut up* stage?"

"We *done* been at the *shut up* stage."

"Oh, right, you're black now too."

"Since you like math: I'm a quarter African, a quarter Indian, a quarter French, a quarter Jew, a quarter Basque."

"Wish you'd told me any of this."

"Hi, my name is Sylvia and I'm in the upstairs hallway of your house and I'm black and will marry a man you don't know and won't like when you do, and your stepfather whom you will try to kill is my father, pleased to make your acquaintance."

"Do you love him?"

"You disappear for two months and ask me that?"

Karl had always assumed it was other people who disappeared.

"Why are you marrying him?"

She abruptly stepped toward Karl, startling him, and thrust her arms to her sides as if to throw the reason she'd agreed to marry Stony down and break it on the forest floor. She stepped back, crossed her arms again, gripped her elbows tight.

"Don't tell my father."

"Why?"

"Don't tell my mother, if you see her."

"Why are you marrying him?"

"I'm pregnant."

He looked down at his body as if to find the hole the news had made in it. He looked back up at her.

"Put your arms down," he said.

Two seconds later, when it occurred to her to protest, she had already obeyed him. She was wearing just a plain old white T-shirt now, but, like anything she wore, it was imbued with Sylvianess. This happened not just with things that were on her but also with things that were near her, like the trees that were behind her, and, from Karl's vantage, visually touched her.

"May I touch it?"

" 'It'?"

"The pregnancy—the baby—the fetus—your belly."

Her answer was to stand still and look away. He slowly brought his palm to rest on the newly swelled place between her sternum and navel. It was softer and warmer than he expected any part of her to be. He was gelatinous, and trembled. He removed his hand, stepped back, and tried to gather himself into himself. He looked in the general vicinity of his feet, which also included Sylvia's cut-off jeans, her luminous and muscular calves, her dirt-edged toes, green flip-flops, mulch, twigs, dirt.

"You're marrying him because you're pregnant? What is this, 1950?"

"No, if this were 1950 he'd set me up in a little slum apartment far away from him and send me monthly checks through a third party. Or he'd have me killed. Anyway, I didn't say I'm marrying him *because* I'm pregnant. That's only part of it."

"What's the other part?"

"Even if I told you all the ostensible reasons, that wouldn't fully explain it."

"How stupid!" Karl looked desperately up at the sky, which the thick green canopy of leaves prevented him from seeing except in isolated shards. "Do you even like me?"

"What's that got to do with anything?"

"A lot!"

"Yes!"

"More than him?"

"I don't like him!"

"Why not?"

"He's gross."

"That may be true, but, objectively, he's of a higher value than I am in almost every category of desirability: height, handsomeness, hair length and texture, physical strength, real estate holdings, fanciness of car, confidence—"

"So why don't *you* marry him?"

"You beat me to it."

"You are truly a moron."

"Exactly, and he's not a moron."

"He's creepy!"

"Okay, so he's not great in the morals department, there's one little strike against him, but I'm not much better."

"You're a lot better."

"I nearly killed your father."

"He deserved it."

She raised her eyebrows then, cinematically, as her father often did. Some unknown, unhappy feeling had entered her, and now it leapt across the forest air from her to him. The soft white birch trees that came up from behind her head had it in them too, and the furry blur of forest green that touched her arms' soft skin.

"I'm sad," he said.

"I know."

"No, I mean that's the only thing you've ever said you like about me, but it's only being depressed that prevents me from being as active a crumb-bum as him: too much effort. "

"That's not true."

"Is there *anything* else you like about me?"

"Oh, my sweet boy!" She leapt, as her unhappiness had done not long before, across the small swath of forest air between them, and took him in her arms. He surrendered to her, and to her chrysanthemum-anxiety smell. She slowly kissed his forehead and his cheek with that ecosystem, her mouth.

"So don't marry him. I mean, come on, where's the logic?"

"This isn't a geometric proof, Karl. There's no QED that precedes a big decision. The bigger the decision, the less logical it probably is."

"Change your mind."

"I can't. There're about twelve things making me do this, and in between the twelve things there's glue gluing them together, and gluing me to him and to the decision to marry him."

"I can't tell if you're bullshitting both yourself and me or just me."

"Let me put it like this. When you were *bludgeoning my dad*, could you have stopped?"

"But you just said . . . That is completely different. That was an impulsive act that took a split second."

"Well, some impulsive acts that take a split second last a lot longer than others."

"That doesn't make sense."

"Again you're trying to measure human behavior with the ruler of 'sense.' "

"Try to explain it to me anyway."

"Our whole lives take a split second, in geological time."

"That would be relevant if we were rocks."

"I wish we were, then this all wouldn't hurt so much."

"What are the eleven other reasons?"

"Maybe there aren't twelve."

"How many then?"

"Man, are you not listening?"

"What are some of the other reasons? What's one other reason?"

"I'm—embroiled. It's complicated."

"Everything with you is."

"Yes! But I see a way out of it."

"To marry him."

"That's part of it."

"All explanations are partial with you."

"Yes."

"But all will be revealed in time, I suppose."

"Never all. Will you be our witness?"

"In Krüog, next Saturday?"

"Yes."

"You want me to bear witness but not tell anyone."

"Not tell *them*."

"Why then?"

"It will help me."

"How?"

"Immeasurably."

"Okay."

"You'll do it?"

"Shit."

The tops of the trees above swayed in a passing breeze and their thousand rattling and rubbing leaves made a noise almost like rain. She placed her hand on his cheek, began to massage his scalp with her fingertips. He stepped away.

"That's a little much for me right now."

"Have you had lunch?" she said.

"No."

"I'll make you some."

"Do you think it's weird that your parents got back together?"

"Yes."

"This is Stony's baby you're pregnant with, right?"

"Duh."

NINE

HE HAD A WICKED STOMACHACHE. His suit was hot,
stiff, tight, and rough against his soft skin. Both his ties were stained.
He paced the byways of his room and thought of men in suits in
their rooms, men leaving buildings they owned to accomplish unpleasant tasks in buildings owned by other men or by companies
or towns. Could an abstract concept own a concrete object? His
tight suit, though none of it was on his head per se, constricted his
thoughts. Against prayers Karl thought he'd uttered with sufficient
clarity and force, Larchmont Jones interrupted his flight from the
house.

"Where you going?"

"Ronkonkoma."

"What for?"

"Date."

He was moving eastward on the lawn, halfway to his car, a pale
brown blob in a field of green. Dew darkened the scuffed sides of
his mass-produced brown shoes.

"This must be some important date. You usually deliberate on
the threshold for a while, even when you're late for work."

Karl wondered if when the manager of the Malaysian factory
Jones employed heard Jones's voice on the phone or saw Jones's

form darken his factory door, he felt the Malaysian equivalent of *Fuck off* rising in him.

He turned to look at his stepfather for the five thousandth time, hoping to use this morning's increased susceptibility to conclude the backbreaking work of resolving the meaning of this man, to obviate the need to look at him, to make all future looking optional. That Jones had on a new maroon silk shirt, that his goatee had turned white and climbed the sides of his blue-gray face, that he would continue to age and get sick and die, that Karl himself would age, that his own aging would alter the meaning of people and objects and memories did not bode well for the resolution Karl sought. And he didn't seek it all that much because be careful of wishing for closure, you might get it.

"I've got an important day coming up soon too, you know," Jones said.

"Great, I look forward to hearing about that."

The summer sun was up above the rooftop of the house across the street. Jones, with the maroon shirt and a mysterious pair of navy trousers, warmed himself in it, leaning semi-borscht-belt style on the doorjamb. *I am leaning amusedly on the doorjamb*, his posture said. Backlit on the spangled lawn, Karl took it in. Did the man know he arched his eyebrows many times each day? Did he arch them when alone? All the exaggerated and mildly to intensely aggressive gestures, remarks, and actions formed a hard cocoon of caricature inside which the uncongealed inner Jones could carry on its indefinite gestation. The cocoon was not a perfect system of protection. Karl's own cocoon was not his personality, because he didn't have one, but his house, because his house was, let's face it, his mother, and when he left his mother or his house he was exposed to grave and unpredictable inconvenience.

He got in the Volvo. How many times had he been in the Volvo? Nine hundred twelve. He joined the pilgrims driving eastward toward the sea.

The name Krüog was a mistake, or so he recalled from a book or a talk. In the 1640s, a group of English settlers had arrived at the place, a fragrant hill between two brooks on the southern fork of Long Island's eastern end, and took a meeting with the local chief around a fire. By signs, they asked him what the place was called. He did not understand, or understood and chose, as 320 years later U.S. Secretary of Defense Robert McNamara would repeatedly do, to answer not the question they had asked but the one he had wanted to hear, which was, "May we stay indefinitely?" The word *no* in the Shinnecock tongue sounded to English ears like *Krüog*, a word which until that time had existed in no language, and so the place became known to whites, and to Indians of a resigned or ironic cast of mind, and eventually to anyone who'd heard of it. Thus did a mistake become a concrete fact and prime vacation spot.

Krüog Town Hall was a simple, honest box of gray-brown weathered wood with A-frame roof, or so Karl remembered being told by that man or book. He was curious about the implication that inanimate objects might also be dishonest, and periodically when encountering one he tried to figure out if it was telling the truth. He had wondered briefly too if, for a man-made object to be honest, everyone involved in its making had to be, and had concluded that that was too stringent a requirement, since some man-made objects were honest but no men were all the time; lying to oneself and others about oneself, others, and the very nature of reality was intrinsic to humans, just as flight was intrinsic to buzzards, and buzzards who busted a wing, like humans who woke up one day to the pure truth, perished quickly unless lovingly maintained in captivity.

Krüog Town Hall had begun its life as a Puritan church in 1641, was burned to the ground by the Dutch in 1673, rebuilt, burned again in 1777 by the Americans, and built again on the same plan ten years later as a dry goods store, which it remained until 1929 when, rendered desperate and insane by the loss of his fortune in the stock market, its then-owner burned himself alive in the place with a single match and a gallon of kerosene. It was rebuilt once more in the 1930s by the Works Progress Administration, and had been the town hall since its completion.

Karl thought Stony might be desperate and insane, deprived not of his fortune but of Sylvia's love, and was burning down his own life and hers by coercing her to marry him—by what means Karl had yet to know. As if to show that marriage equaled death, she wore powder on her face that emphasized its already notable pallor, and on the great soft topography of her lips a shade of red tinged with corpse-blue. Her linen dress was midnight blue and hugged her form, not least the small, swelling hillock of her belly. He wondered how many rules of this particular arrangement he had been summoned to witness were codified, how many written down by the two parties, how many spoken, how many had been and would be ardently contested as need for them arose in bride or groom, each contest ending in the bitter defeat of one and the bitter triumph of the other.

In the anteroom to the judge's chambers, bride and groom sat side by side on a hardwood bench and held hands, he with a show of comfort and jovial affection, she with an air of hostile sorrow—which is to say, like a real couple. Stony's creamy brown suit was also of linen, and seemed made by the same man who'd made

Sylvia's dress, being possessed of a similar forthright elegance, now that Karl was bent on assessing the relative honesty of made things. Arv, who sat next to Karl on an identical bench across from the couple, rounded out the wedding party. He wore a powder blue polyester tux with black piping and ruffled shirt, a suit not dishonest but either brilliantly satirical or oblivious. His rubbery face was the battleground for platoons of feelings caused perhaps on this day by his adoration of the groom and his execration of the bride. Karl craned his neck to look at Arv; Arv craned his neck to look at Karl; each blanched and retreated to himself with a new unhappy thought.

They were led into a small room in which a brown woman in a black robe sat behind a tan desk. With an impassive nod suggesting justice was not blind but bored, she moved them to the chairs before the desk. Quiet time ensued. Stony sat relaxedly. Sylvia's hands squeezed her chair's arms. Arv fidgeted. Karl spied an oak tree in the yard and climbed it with his eyes. The judge looked down at papers on her desk. The wedding had begun. Though the law was everywhere, it inhered densely in the law books on the shelves behind the judge, in the papers she now looked at on the desk, in the desk, in her robe, in her body: silence, time, books, papers, desk, judge, and room congealed in a superviscous concentrate of law. She began to say the wedding words. It had not occurred to Karl that people could be married sitting down. The wrongness of this union was not to be adjudicated by the law this room and judge were vessels of. His hope remained therefore with racial telepathy: the judge would sense her sister Sylvia's distress by Negroid mind-meld; she would know through the place in her body where ancestral fellow feeling dwelled that this wedding must not come to pass because this sister did not love the heartless white man seated to her right in his coffee-and-cream linen suit, but the doleful white man seated to her left in his babyshit wool one. Indeed, this did happen in the world that went no farther than the inner wall of Karl's skull.

The judge neared the point of no return while Karl, who was definitely not that good at always paying attention to what was happening right in front of him, climbed with his sad black baby eagle's eyes to the topmost branch of the oak tree out the window, clung to it with stick-thin talons, and did not hear the judge's ". . . speak now or forever hold your peace," but heard instead the wind in the air and the songs of his fellow birds who, it must be said in their favor, would never marry.

There followed a wedding luncheon at the large old home of Stony Stonington during which Karl attempted to discover what he was supposed to be doing. House, job, house, job, car, until recently, had been allowed by Karl more than by most to constitute the parameters of his life—to stand in for it—adding, ancillarily, a couple dozen books a year; twenty times that many masturbations, some rueful, some less so; and those engagements with other people, primarily Larchmont Jones, that made up the slings and arrows of ordinary fortune—Karl having thought, till now, that the outrageous fortune part of his life was behind him. And that thought had been a species of optimism, he realized with surprise, and with dismay that he'd used what was probably his life's allotment of optimism on a premise contradicted by nearly all of experience.

Stony had removed his suit jacket to reveal the full grandeur of his soft, white, porous, flowing linen shirt. He spoke indulgently of his wife's adamant stipulation that the wedding party consist only of the four people now present. He stood behind a chair and leaned relaxedly on its wooden back in his enormous Krüog dining room. He did or seemed to do everything relaxedly, malice pouring off of him in waves. Karl experimented with the concept that his purpose at the lunch was to disrupt his host's relaxedness and that that would be his purpose on earth till Stony wasn't relaxed anymore, and though he had no gift for disruption or plan for how to accomplish it, it became for now a notional hat to replace the actual one Stony had absconded with.

When Karl said, "I'd like my hat back now, please," and Sylvia replied, "Really? That's all you can think of now is your dumbass hat?" mirth rose up Stony's formidable body and came to rest in his honey-colored eyes. He seemed to love the discomfiture of his new wife. Or maybe he loved being in his dining room, and the hard wife he'd populated it with, just as he'd populated her with his heir, brought the needed drama to a room whose size, shape, and furnishings he'd selected as a stage set for it. Karl groaned, and Stony smiled as if he owned the sound, having purchased it not with money but with the acuity about people's desires that had enabled him to acquire the money. He continued to stand at the head of the table and lean on the wooden chair back. Sylvia, a bolt of lightning in a sealed jar, dashed up and down the table's length by the windows. Beyond the windows were a thick, tall, kempt lawn, a few pine trees with soft red bark, and a placid cove. Upon their arrival at the house, Stony had described the cove as a series of Impressionist paintings of water, clouds, and light, but the cove was the agent the sea had sent to reclaim the man who thought he owned the house, and so for that matter were the clouds. Clouds might look like people but would never really be them, whereas people would eventually be clouds.

So much to absorb in this big dining room and Karl would have liked a moment's rest from absorption to figure out what to do. Like right now he was thinking this huge house on the shore, this millionaire's mansion on the island's posh east end was the kind of place Larchmont Jones often told him he'd have liked to move to when Karl's mom was sick, but being in this dining room, being encased in this sumptuously furnished, open-windowed mausoleum on this fine summer day of his doom enabled Karl to know that his stepdad could never have afforded such a place, and when exposed to the actual house of Stony, the fantasy house of Jones that Jones and Karl had made in Karl crumbled. This crumbled thing joined other crumbled things in him, where each day brought new destruction.

Arv was there too, of course. The Arvs of the world stay home less than one would like. He was seated at one of the table's two long flanks, near its head, beside his pal, across from Karl. Behind him were the windows and the agitated Sylvia. His beige cloth napkin, which he had tucked into his collar, covered his bow tie and ruffled shirt front. The sunlight pouring in through the windows semiblinded Karl and obscured Arv's rough features; Arv seemed to be begging and panting and making his upraised hands into paws. He barked. Karl understood or thought he understood that Arv was mocking Stony's doglike hunting of and also submission to his new bride, a gloss in mimicry on the saying *All men are dogs.* This was a very good dog impression. It lightened Karl's heavy heart. His body softened up by mirth, he reconsidered Arv, or maybe just considered him. Sylvia had moved to the pantry and stood stock still in Karl's line of sight, her athletic muscle tone hardened into brittleness. She stared at Karl. He went to her.

"I'm about to give my toast," Stony said with the mock distress of a father who will enjoy his children's unruliness only up to a point, and then will be enraged by it.

The pantry was a vestibule between the dining room and kitchen with floor-to-ceiling shelves on which wet food was stored in jars and dry food in boxes and tins. The shapes of the jars and their labels and the boxes' graphic designs were strange to Karl, artisanal and refined, signaling ingredients grown, raised, processed, and prepared with a degree of loving attention that put the resulting food above his pay grade.

Sylvia's face was close to his. Her body made the air vibrate. "You're not supposed to be enjoying this, you know."

"Oh, really? Tell me not just to show up at this abortion but exactly how to feel about it. Totally relieve me of the burden of autonomy."

She giggled, a quiet and abbreviated expression of genuine pleasure from a woman certain her misfortune was not yet at its worst.

"What?" he said.

"I love when you get indignant."

In the warmth of the pantry he saw that she'd removed her high heels, that they'd left red ridges on the tops of her feet, that on her wedding day her feet were not clean, that they gripped the floor as her pale, taut skin gripped the air, that her blue dress was wet, that she was a pregnant animal trapped in a pantry. Jellies, jams, chutneys, sauces, pickled things, pasta, bread, flour, coffee, tea, cereal, crackers, cookies, bags of onions and potatoes swirled around him in the tiny room.

"You know who's interesting?" he said.

"Who?"

"Arv."

"Arv's horrid."

"That may be, but he's complex."

"Who said he wasn't?"

"I give most people little credit for complexity."

"That's because people scare you and you stay sealed up in your house to avoid them." She cooed this criticism directly into his ear as if it were a lullaby. From his ear, the warmth traveled inward and downward.

"Arv's barking was a soliloquy," Karl whispered back, "about how life disappoints him, knowledge eludes him, and the strong triumph over the weak regardless of either's virtue."

They glanced toward the dining room, where Stony hit Arv on the snout with a rolled-up magazine and Arv whined.

"Arv is vile," she said.

"He's harmless."

"He's the one who put a mickey in your drink at the party."

"What's a mickey?"

"A roofie."

"What's a roofie?"

"Date rape drug. Don't look like that, no one raped you. But Arv drove you to the beach in your own car while you were still unconscious and dumped you on the sand."

"Why?"

"Because he's vile. You can't protect me if you're clueless."

"And why weren't you protecting me the night of the party?"

"I was vomiting. My morning sickness came at night."

"Was I supposed to stop the wedding? Is that how I was supposed to protect you?"

"No, I had to marry him."

"So you keep insisting."

"I need you to figure out how to protect me."

"So, protect you by figuring out how to protect you."

"Yes."

Her face was inches from his. She looked at him with pleading in her eyes. He put his hand on her cheek and she held it there with her hand.

Stony, who was leaning in the doorway of the pantry, said, "The groom would like to give his toast now, lovebirds."

What was one to think of his toast, especially if one was not really paying attention to it? One mainly heard its tone, which was tender, jovial, calm, and therefore demented and terrifying. He insisted she make one too. "Wow, marriage, glad that's over with, cheers," was hers, more or less. They drank. White waitstaff brought food none ate. They drank more though. "Bathroom!" Karl cried, and left. His real goal was his hat. He wandered up a wide flight of stairs. He found a room with a bed and a window and looked at the water and thought of his mother. She had married Larchmont Jones. Teen Karl went to the wedding but teen Vetch did not, or so she claimed. He must have seen her somewhere though. If he'd known himself he'd have noticed her and would remember her. Where were the sensations a person had had and not noticed? And might he not remember his mother because she too had been unformed? He thought of her photo in the college yearbook, in the days before the advent of the peasant blouse, glasses too big for her face, dark hair straightened with that era's crude machine, a large blob of false straightness arcing down her head on either side, the clouded look in her eye of a girl who could not unite her perceptions and thoughts with the organizing principle of an integrated

MATTHEW SHARPE

self. Marriage for such a one was always blackmail of a kind. He
stayed in his house to stay with his out-of-it homemaker mom,
and stayed dead to stay close to her via resemblance.

He felt the flesh of another human on his back and arms and
neck. It hurt. Some part of him behind his head was being stretched
beyond comfort.

"Hello, Karl." That was Stony.

"What are you doing?"

"What are *you* doing?"

"Looking for my hat."

"It's not here. You missed Arv's toast, and didn't make one yourself. This hold is called a full nelson. It can be used as a neck crank
where the head can be pushed into positions past its normal rota-
tion, causing hyperextension of the spine. USA Wrestling, which is
the governing body of wrestling in America, has banned it but they
teach it anyway at wrestling camps from coast to coast. Wrestling
coaches are a strange lot, all those muscles are the male equivalent
of hysteria. You could stomp on my foot or break my knee with
your heel but by the time you did I'd have dislocated both your
arms or snapped your spinal cord." Stony moved Karl to the bed
and leaned forward. Karl fell facedown and Stony fell on top of
him. Stony's cheek of muscle and bone pressed against Karl's one
of loose flesh. There was wetness on Karl's cheek as well, his forehead, nose, and mouth were mashed into the bedspread's textured
nubs, his legs pinned by Stony's legs. "We're in each other's lives
now, but there are some places you can't go, and this is one of them.
If you come to the second floor of my house again without being
invited you'll find yourself in this same position, only your pants
will be down and I'll be raping you."

Karl realized seemingly for the first time that when he'd discov-

132

ered Sylvia in his house nine weeks ago, she and Stony had quite recently had sex. And you may wonder if Karl was a virgin. He was not. He had had intercourse three times in college with a girl in a dorm down the street from his; once each with two whores, not liking johndom the first time and confirming he didn't like it the second; he'd paid seven women from three continents to stroke his penis on eight occasions in two years; and had not had nonsolitary sex of any kind in five. Three, one, one, two, seven, three, eight, two, five: he liked to do the numbers in his head and by counting know himself.

The two men lay quietly. To get what little air he could Karl had to smile or sneer with the left side of his mouth, the side away from Stony's hard cheek. The situation taken as a whole was not as unpleasant as he'd have thought. Stony had charisma, money, intelligence, confidence, and handsomeness, that is, as he had said to Sylvia, excellence across a spectrum of attributes not including virtue. He was not a good man but good men's goodness was often just embarrassing to Karl. This guy was not a bore to be around. Something interesting was always about to happen in his company. Capitulation—not to any man but to him—had a soothing quality that reminded Karl of home.

He preceded Stony down the stairs. "That wasn't so bad," the latter said.

Arv had spread the sports page on the naked tablecloth and was lost in it.

"Arv is a beautiful reader of a sports section. He do the coaches in different voices."

"Where's Sylvia?"

The name caused Arv to flinch as if slapped.

She appeared at the pantry door. "Mets won, pay up, chump."

"No." Arv slammed the paper shut.

"Arv, you welching on my wife?"

"I have no money."

"I'll garnish your wages."

"You garnished them last week."

The lunch wound down. All were in sour moods but the groom, who did not have moods. Stony told the startled help, "Have the dishes those two ate off of"—indicating Arv and Karl—"destroyed." An overnight stay in tents in a local wood was spoken of by groom, bride, and Arv, to one another and to Karl, in a way that made clear it had been discussed in full with Karl even though he did not remember that and did not want to go. He was made to see he'd agreed to camp, which entailed a trip with Arv to Arv's to pick up gear while bride and groom were left alone, another horrifying thought in a series.

Little must be said of the trip to Arv's. His japes on general topics and his jibes against the bride would have been enjoyable if Karl didn't hate them. He'd almost have rather been alone.

In the late afternoon the two passed in Karl's car beneath the wooden entrance sign of Mashumup Nature Preserve, on which a wag had painted "Abandon all hope, you who enter here," and another or the same wag had painted "Nature *macht frei*." Karl let Arv haul all the stuff. They walked away from the graveled and gently shaded parking lot and past the empty, locked, nostalgic cabin that served as the nature preserve's headquarters, on their way presumably to its hindquarters. As they entered the tunnel of trees, gravel gave way to twigs and dirt, and their sounds diminished down to the soft clump of mass-produced rubber soles on warmed summer earth. The tree world enveloped them and Karl tried not to forget to let the gentle smell and soft green tree light go deep in him, and suffered as he failed in this. When did he need tree balm more than now?

Stony was putting up the two-man tent in which he and his new wife would lie that night. His back to the arrivals, he squatted and tied a stake to a tent flap with thin rope, the muscles and veins in relief on his elegant arms. Karl was to share a tent with Arv, whose seemingly infinite mediocrity made him at once familiar and mysterious.

"Sylvia's waiting for you down by the cove," Stony said without turning away from his work.

"Me?" Karl said.

"You."

Karl lingered at Stony's back.

"You're dismissed."

Karl walked down the path to the beach as the sun made its final leisurely descent into the sea. The moon had risen early and now rested white-faint and indifferent in the purpling sky. Seagulls yo-yoed slowly up and down at water's edge, dropping scallops on the rocks, retrieving them, and so on, lamenting the tedium of this limited routine with their high-pitched mews, like a flock of kittens trapped in a dark shoebox.

Sylvia sat upon a rock at the shore. Her muscular back pressed against her pale blue sweatshirt. She and Stony belonged to the corporeal aristocracy. She'd made a lot of noise about how much sorrow this union caused her, and he did not think she was lying, but her resistance to her groom was just a part of how such things were meant to go: young, fine, energetic people like her in whom nature had concentrated its gifts had to resist, had to pass neck-deep through a thick and stinking swamp, which was their own disgust with the unfairness of said gifts, before they entered the kingdom of their destiny and took their place on its throne, which in Sylvia's case was in hand-holding range of Stony's throne.

Karl sat beside her on the rock. She took his hand, kissed it, squeezed it to her breastbone, which hurt him. She let it go and put hers gently on his knee. They were silent. The soft sweet smell of salt and gentle vegetable decay came in from the bay while what may have been jasmine drifted down on the air from the woods. The seagulls moved off to the south; their hard complaint turned distant and sad, like a major loss vaguely recalled. A cricket chirped, then three, then ten. Low bay waves washed up in slow spondees. Evening and evening of the heart arrived at once.

She removed her hand from his knee and looked at him and raised her eyebrows as if their beloved and clownish uncle had just died in his early sixties of congestive heart failure and what was there to do?

"Arv twisted his ankle on the trail and fell down with all the gear on his back. I didn't stop to help him," Karl said.

"Don't waste your conscience on him."

"The conscience is not a finite resource."

"Yes it is."

Karl felt Sylvia was revealing important information about herself in this remark, which, if he only knew the proper way to hear it, would yield the solution to the mystery of her. And even if, as she herself would say, a personality was not a math problem, he knew there was something crucial he had not yet understood about her—just to limit the field, for the moment, of world phenomena he had not yet understood something crucial about.

"So what," he said, "if I were to have lent a jerk a helping hand and he'd repaid me with further jerkiness, so what?"

"To call him a jerk is to underestimate his power to do harm. Trust me."

"Trust you. I can't be in my room, I can't be in my house, my yard, I can't be on my sidewalk or in my town without feeling them as places you've touched—with—your skin. You've now married this man you claim to loathe and won't tell me why. You *heap* on me decisions and requests I'm meant to take on faith, and now you want me to trust your dire assessment of this goofball over my own mild one without, again, offering a single reason why I should except that you are telling me to. I won't do it. I won't do it!"

The sun went down and she sighed. Flat, bloodred clouds lay in jagged stripes at earth's edge.

"I have explained some things to you," she said. "But no, you're right. This is why I need you. You're more decent than I am, and trusting."

"I'm not that trusting."

"And I've abused your trust not by lying to you—"

"You *have* lied to me, a number of times."

"—but by asking too much of you. You've a core goodness that you somehow weirdly assert despite your passivity."

"I know, I'm so passive, ugh!"

"I want to spend time with you. I want to be with you. You make me think about hard things. You might even one day make me nicer although that would be truly scary because niceness seems to me kind of like this baby field mouse with a broken leg just waiting out in the middle of nowhere to have its neck snapped and be devoured."

Stony and nighttime arrived simultaneously. "That was beautiful," the former said. "We're all in a reflective mood now. We're all philosophical now in this beautiful place that money can't buy on the night of the nuptials. It smells so delicious here, I'm invigorated. Let's forgive each other our trespasses. I forgive you both."

"For what?" they said.

"Oh, *come* on," Stony said in either mock disgust or disgust. Karl respected Stony's use of tonal ambiguity as a method of intimidation.

Sylvia stood up and walked away before they could stop her. The two men were alone in the woods in the dark of night, Karl on his ass on a rock, Stony on his feet behind him. Karl stood, removed a miniature flashlight from his pocket, and turned it on.

"That was smart of you to bring that," Stony said. "May I have it?"

"No."

Stony took the flashlight from Karl's hand and pressed down so violently on his shoulder that Karl sat back down on the rock.

"I dislike you. You're demented. I love the woman you just married and she loves me and she doesn't love you. You coerced her."

"She doesn't love you. You're effectively a child, and not even a promising child with an interesting hobby like cello playing. You possess no innate talent or virtue or forcefulness."

"She may not love me but she likes me. She doesn't like you."

"She may not like me but she loves me."

"She doesn't love you, she despises you."

"She may despise me but she continues to fuck me."

"You really should not say just anything that pops into your head. It's impolite." Karl stood, spat in Stony's eye, ran away in the dark across the rocks, and fell on his face.

Stony was upon him. "This is different now from this afternoon in the bedroom in a number of ways. You've spat on me and verbally insulted me. We are alone on a beach at the edge of a forest. I have used my connections in town government to get a permit to camp here even though they never issue permits to camp here, so there's no one around for miles. Now I'm just going to place my—uh, sorry, *your* flashlight on the pebbles here like so, pointed at your hand and, as you can see, my knife. I've tried different brands but I come back to the Swiss Army Knife for its elegance and utility. Let's make a little test first."

Stony made a light slice perpendicular to Karl's right pinkie finger just below its middle knuckle. He was somehow holding Karl's hand down by the wrist. Karl felt the hard pebbles on the underside of his wrist and palm, and the sting of the slice, and saw, thanks to the flashlight, the thin red line of blood.

"I don't know," Stony said, "how many slices it will take to get all the way through the finger. This is reasonable recompense, I think, for what you've said and done, for how profoundly you've interfered with my happiness. You might say I'm plaintiff, judge, jury, and, as it were, executioner here. You might say it's un-American of me not to abide by the legal division of labor that assures justice. What would the nice lady who married us today say about this punishment? 'I'm sorry he made you unhappy, Mr. Stonington. I'm sorry he ruined the one thing in your life that could have brought you true happiness, but that still does not constitute adequate justification for cutting off his finger, here in America. Here in America, amputation is not considered a reasonable punishment for anything. You will not find precedent for it in any law book, though you'll no doubt find that elsewhere—in the street, perhaps, or in the wild.' And that is where we are now, Karl. And really, right now, I feel *in the wild*, don't you?"

Karl did feel in the wild too, here where the Dutch and the English and the Indians had exacted justice from one another plentifully and with minimal interference from or recourse to the laws that had bound each but not all. And that may have been why he also felt resigned to losing this relatively unimportant appendage. "Not long from now, this will have happened," he felt, but Stony was not cutting, he was making a noise with his mouth. His mouth was open and a shapeless sound emerged from it, a nonlanguage sound, something between coughing and singing. Weeping, Karl eventually decided.

"Damn it! It's not even—" He wept and tried to control it and could not, all the while pressing Karl's wrist into the pebbles of the beach with what turned out to be his knee. Karl relaxed while Stony got the cry out of his system and Karl wished he would quit trying to stop himself from crying because that just delayed the release of Karl's wrist from Stony's knee.

"It's not even empathy," Stony finally said. "I don't think it is. And it's not cowardice. It's not caution. I think it's discouragement. Don't flatter yourself that you've discouraged me, Karl. *She* has."

Stony stood up and Karl stood up. His wrist was bruised, if not broken. There were abrasions elsewhere on his body that he could not properly locate.

"I've behaved abominably and it's not even been worth it. I don't mean to say that I've not behaved abominably before—I have, and have been quite conscious of it, and that's why it's paid off, because I've measured it out—I'll cause *this* much suffering in *this* circumstance for *this* outcome—and so I always got what I set out for, but not this time. Not yet, anyway. That's a warning to you that I haven't given up. I just need to figure out how not to be destroyed by her. That's a real conundrum. Now that we're having this brief cease-fire, this moment in the beautiful woods where we're just being humans together, will you please corroborate—are you and I not now brought together here in this pastoral setting because you *can* corroborate—that she simply is able to fuck a man to pieces?"

Karl was too distraught to corroborate this or even to know he could not. He bent down and picked up the flashlight and trained it on the trail back to the makeshift campsite and walked away from Stony, who had begun to cry again on an open vowel, hands at his sides, freely and unselfconsciously, a very tall three-year-old with magnificent posture and long, luxuriant hair, a perfect being giving full expression to a pure sentiment. He caught up with Karl and took the flashlight from him and threw him to the ground and marched off ahead of him down the trail.

Arv grumblingly scoured the camping pot of frank 'n' bean residue by the fire. How scary could a man be about whom one so readily wanted to say, "Good ol' Arv," even or especially in times of tribulation? Arv with his rubbery nose and tight dark curls, was he a Negress too, at this point? Nothing is but what is not, Karl vaguely recalled someone having said.

"There's food for you on that plate," Arv said in annoyance as Karl approached. "It's a little encrusted but that's wilderness camping for you."

"Where're Sylvia and Stony?"

"Stony didn't eat and Sylvia did, she's pregnant."

"Did I ask you if they'd eaten?"

"They went to their tent."

"Great."

"You axed, girlfriend."

Karl sat across the fire from Arv and tried to eat his cold franks 'n' beans. No light came from or penetrated the marriage tent. Light, harsh whispers and swishing of fabric reached Karl's ears.

"Do we have music?" he asked.

" 'Have' in what sense?"

"In the sense of fuck you."

"No."

"Tell a joke or something."

"Two idiots go camping with a pair of newlyweds. One of them says, 'Do we have any music?' The other says, 'No soap radio.' "

"I'm going to bed."

Karl ducked inside the little raincoat-material tent and semi-disrobed and slid into the borrowed sleeping bag that had a mushroomy Arv smell around which Karl hastily hammered together a rickety fence of inattention. Arv came in and seemed to settle right into juicy sleep breaths. It was not much past nine P.M. Karl lay on his back trying not to think or smell or hear or feel, trying to be as little Karl as he could and meld with the local molecules, though he melded no less tentatively than he did not meld.

For how many minutes or hours had this passive struggle gone on before he heard the first of a particular set of outdoor sounds, a grunt, of probably a creature indigenous to Suffolk County? Grunting, regular grunting, rhythmic grunting and breathing not from the county at large but from the next tent over—low, harsh whispers and rasping breaths and light smacks and a sharp high vocal noise—a yip—and soft insistent percussive sounds of cloth or skin or flesh or bone on barely cushioned earth. Love sounds. Not love sounds, sex sounds, hard sounds, mean—not rape—rough sex. Karl screamed. He thought he'd screamed but hadn't, wanted to and didn't. The scream was strong in him and he had to hold it back all the way down his body. He knew that a great deal was predicated on his not screaming exactly now, that this may well have been the core of the task she needed him along on the honeymoon to accomplish—to be here now, for this, and not scream.

TEN

THE EARTH MOISTENED and steamed like a febrile sheep-dog. Karl slept and ate and read a book about George Boole, a nineteenth-century Englishman who'd thought up a useful system wherein algebraic concepts could be used to make logical propositions about the world. So, for example, if the totality of the world was represented by the number one, and the letter x represented the adjective *horned*, then $(1-x)$ would represent all non-horned things, or the experience of at least thinking about them, a mental operation that without the aid of mathematical principles and symbols would have been impossible. Karl had long enjoyed performing this operation in his spare time—if one may speak of "spare" time—in the way that a person can be consoled by the reliability of assertions as true as they are useless. But just at the moment when he'd found a vital use for Boolean logic, its value had fallen off sharply, for let us say that y—and the letter was not chosen at random—equals the proper name *Sylvia*, and, to restrict the field further for precision's sake, not Sylvia as denoting all things living or otherwise that went by that name, but specifically the one who had recently married Charles "Stony" Stonington in Krüog. Boolean logic ought to have been able to assure us that the phrase $(1-y)$ could represent all non-Sylvia things, but as was adumbrated not long ago in Mashumup at dusk by Karl to γ, his findings repeatedly showed that Boolean logic could superduper not account for the way in which so many presumably non-Sylvia things had become Sylvia things without strictly *being* Sylvia, as for example the air, or the moon, which, when he watched it diminish in size from one night to the next, made him feel he was losing her by a corresponding increment. George Boole had been born to the working classes, had devoted his life to the pursuit of truth, and had nonetheless drowned in the fluid of his own lungs at age forty-nine.

Karl sunbathed once with Arv and fished with him once. They joked. Sylvia, increasingly fat, came by twice, yelled at her father, dragged Karl by the arm into the yard and whispered things to him of great urgency that he barely made sense of and could not remember once she'd left—to do with money, he guessed, and real estate, areas of inquiry more abstract for him than the equations which during the school year were his daily bread. Once a week there was an excruciating luncheon for four at the Stonington residence.

The planet moved around the sun. Geologic time lurched ahead. Karl too. *Tick, tick, boom*, a song on the radio said; Karl knew it referred to him but not how. There came a tougher lunch than all the ones before, hours long, unleavened by Arv. Chef salad, dressing overvinegared, oily chips, bread and butter, pulpy mimosas with airy prosecco, six-figure 3-D wallpaper peeled despite the central AC, grim remarks delivered sublingually, Sylvia's finger in the air—couldn't bring herself to say it, hard feelings made harder. Beyond the window, Stony's home cove might as well have been a painting of a cove, for all it breathed coastal freshness into this stultifying box. A mouse ran along the wall. Stony flung a china plate, sliced the mouse in two, stained the air and then his rug with blood. Karl, drunk and low, wandered home behind the wheel, the hour embalmed in heat and dusk.

A sign of trouble at the Floor-Jones home: the door to the basement steps on the side of the house had been left up, one of that species of prefab wedge-shaped umber metal American basement entrances that looks like a short ramp up which you'd roll at top speed and hit your house's outer wall and die. Karl moved with stealth down his steep and narrow outside basement stairs with a mimosa'd sense of himself as a young man on meaningful stairs on a Saturday of his life in this world. The coolness of the stair environment felt charged with relevance; the concrete basement moss and leafmeal rot, the level of the lawn rising up along his eyes, his hot ears and lips, the fullness of his slack face-flesh all led in with purpose to the rustle and the scrape, the light high groan and shadowed motion in the far dim corner of the underground room. He saw at the edge of the halo of light from the bare ceiling bulb a figure on its knees, face away from Karl and toward the wall. It looked, based on that quick work of the eyes that assesses the meaning of movements and forms, to be engaged in a task requiring effort, focus, and skill. Woodwork came to mind. This person, too—a male, he saw now, with short dark curls—was not the only living creature in that corner of the room. Two pairs of light-haired legs, knees toward the room, stood between the wall and the thing now known to him to be a kneeling boy or man. Light shirts came down to the waists of the standing forms, also male, no pants or underpants in sight. Karl came in quiet and a little to the side, not yet noticed by the three, whom he had now identified, two by face and hair, one by hair and movement style. The ones up top were Paul and Hal, the blond-haired boys from trig who'd savaged him last spring, their comic sneers of scorn eroded as he watched by waves of physical bliss. The one below, of course, a sweet and gentle ton of bricks—all the jokes, the social self nearly overridden with a manner that had seemed to exceed its purpose till now—was Arv, suckling one, milking the other by hand; and switching off; and switching off.

Who was working harder at his job of absorption, Arv or Karl? So many new sensations for the latter to take in: this configuration of bodies, Karl not having seen or done man-man sex to date; a new wrinkle as it were in the amalgam of phenomena that coalesced in Karl under the heading *Arv*; a melancholy tenderness for a man who enjoyed hiding in basements with boys, abasement to boys, and was so eager for a double jolt of underage semen, one in mouth, one in hand, that he'd wreck his knees for this luxury on the rough concrete floor of the excavated room beneath the house of a semiantagonist (unless knee ruin was primary, the two cums ancillary); which softened the additional thought, regarded almost with amusement now by Karl, that it must have been Arv who'd subcontracted out last spring's hit on him by these boys, the order having come from the top of the four-man chain of command.

Hal or Paul—it hardly mattered which—tapped the top of Arv's head. Arv looked up at him. He pointed at their secret observer. Arv craned his neck around, said, "Oh, hi, Karl," and went back to work. The boys from trig gazed languidly at Karl, at each other, shrugged without shrugging, and each returned to the dreamy inspection of his own eyebrows. Feeling it rude to stay till the end, Karl tiptoed back up the outer stairs with the unformed presentiment of having seen something important down there to do with the room or the objects in it quite apart from any penis, hand, or mouth.

In the main body of the house, too, which went by in a quick and still-drunk blur, he vaguely sensed a new quality, an increased spaciousness or dustiness perhaps, whose meaning he did not try to work out before dropping to his side on his bed and letting sleep absolve him of further consideration.

He woke in the dark with an ache in his head and sand in his neck. He went to the bathroom, hosed analgesics and fluids. A lot of physical pain this year and more to come. It was hot in the house. Why would a guy turn off the AC when he knew his stepson would be home later?

He thought of the sights that had whipped by his head on the trip that he took on drunken feet two hours ago across the foyer, up the stairs, down the fateful upstairs hall, and into bed. What had he seen? What had he *not* seen, more like? Well-known objects, some bigger than him. What would two young thugs do after being fellated in the basement of the math teacher they probably knew to be taking a drunken nap? They'd come up the stairs and burgle his stuff. Burgled again, less lovingly this time. The widget on the wall was gone, the one in lucite Jones had made that had paid for the house and for college for Karl. Thanks, widget, bye, fuck you, widget. And the piano, now that Karl was downstairs, was a big thing that was gone. How could two postorgasmic teens and their adult lover carry a baby grand? Could the plan have really been sex in the basement, then up the stairs to void the house while Karl slept?

This might have been a drunken dream—even in sleep he didn't get out of the house much. He hovered in the brief nonarea between the rec room and the living room. More had happened here than one might think. Fierce, prolonged battles for air temperature were waged on the five-inch field of the knob on the wall, which Karl now moved to cool the rooms. His mother, Belinda Floor née Weeks, had stood in this place on five thousand nights and, Scheherazade of brown 'n' serve, called "Dinner" in her soft voice to the nightly succession of Karls who'd played in the rec room or read a book or stared at nothing and thought nothing of consequence. He went to the kitchen, as all men must do, to forage for food: salami, cheese, mustard, bread, olives: mom's milk. A folded piece of paper on the table said, "To my stepson." He read the note in Jones's shaky hand:

> My Dear Man:
>
> How unreachable you have been this summer and always. I wish you or Sylvia—my children—had told me about the wedding. She has made up for this. You have not. No matter. I love you, there, did you know that little detail about me? And it is with love that I say how could you stand by and let Charles Stonington castrate your testicles off? They do grow back in rare cases, maybe you'll get lucky.
>
> With Henrietta Jones, my former wife, I have bought a brownstone in the Clinton Hill section of Brooklyn, address below, and moved there, leaving you, as you can see, with enough furnishings so as not to make you feel denuded. Good luck with the house and all else.
>
> Yours fondly, etc.

That bastard had turned the AC off with malice aforethought. Karl drove to Brooklyn in sweaty brunch clothes with a headache no pill could cure. These long summer nights on the Long Island Expressway were really spooky. A darkness so desolating and profound he felt could not have been native to this land but must have been brought by those who settled it, laid down as an undercoat to this miraculous society predicated on endless combustion, which in turn was predicated on that dark, which even a typical insensible citizen like the one in the Volvo must sometimes feel in those rare, lonely moments on his way from one lit place to the next. Prehuman island life loomed up and pressed in on the lone driver. He rolled down the windows. Air pummeled his face and roared in his ears. Time and more time barreled into the car from the west, was sloughed off, and rolled out to the choppy waters of the Sound. Karl dreamed of his mother again, a little poodly gal this time, a little prissy in her immaculately ironed and bleached white peasant blouse, all things just so, "Dinner" uttered crisply, no one late in my house, finish your broccoli, your handwriting is abominable, it can't have been I who taught you that. She married up and cowed the wealthy man and died. Whoever said the dead are not dead but live in the memories of those who survive them never had a dead mother. The dead die and die again.

He was in Brooklyn now. He did not know the hour, a hot Saturday night. Black people—African-Americans—moved along the sidewalks of Myrtle Avenue in fine summer clothes, limbs and faces double-browned in the luminate marmalade composed of streetlamp glow and incomplete urban nighttime dark. A few pink folks mixed in among the brown, reflecting in colorized miniature, Karl thought, as he rolled down the windows of his russet Volvo, the race mix of the land on which we'd all lived in bodily proximity for centuries. Were not the fierce and jagged rhymes tumbling over steel-reinforced bass and drums on these shop stoops and corners the same ones listened to by clusters of theoretically white high school boys on Saturday nights at the mall in Karl's hometown? *Yo, shorty, how y'all fill tonight?*—who said that, white man or black man? Who said, *Why you hatin'?* Who said, *You see, maybe you's got to be po' a long time fust, en so you might git discourage' en kill yo'self 'f you didn' know by de sign dat you gwyne to be rich bymeby?* Who said, *I was raised with the help of a white grandfather who survived a Depression to serve in Patton's army during World War II and a white grandmother who worked on a bomber assembly line at Fort Leaven-worth while he was overseas?* Who said, *Now all they got to do is make the robot that can walk and talk and kick your motherfuckin' ass?*

He turned right onto the street in question, and seemed to have crossed into another town. The retail jangle and upbeat party vibe of the avenue was gone. Quietude suffused this block of somber homes shielded from the street by wide walks and shallow gated yards. A wide brown church in whose façade bloomed a mon-strous rose of stained glass hugged the walk and lent its stretch of street in muffled form the old-time R&B that played inside its doors.

The doors opened and the sound brightened. Two backlit fig-ures emerged and eased onto the walk, the one holding the other for support and vice versa, like two birds with one wing each, ex-hausted and a mile above the earth. Karl parked and watched them move down the street. She wore a light and wide-brimmed hat, floral dress, shoes with mid-height heels that evidently pained her feet and legs. He had on a Panama, a goatee, a seersucker, Tony Bennetts with no socks.

Karl slipped in behind the two and trailed them for a minute in silence, partly because he had never resolved what name to hail this man by. "Ms. Jones," he finally said.

"What is it, dear?" she asked before she'd turned around.

"Late, unannounced, unasked for, just like at his birth," said the man he had recently killed.

"Monty, saying things like that will not make him less sullen."

"His sullenness level does not determine my remarks."

"Does human decency?" Karl asked.

"He does have an endearing wit," Monty said.

"So you two've moved in together?"

"We've resolved our differences," he said.

She said, "No we haven't."

"Come on in, we'll show you the place."

Jones opened a low black iron gate on a minuscule yard with a small magnolia tree whose period of flowering had long passed; it was unfragrant but healthily leaved. The couple managed the eight stone steps up to the front door singly, slowly, one on the left, one on the right, with the aid of a pair of iron handrails. In the house, cardboard boxes, some open, many not, sat among couches, chairs, the piano. The walls and floors were bare, the lights bright, the air cool and smelling of fresh paint. The owners removed their hats.

"Come into the kitchen. You hungry? You smell bad. You look bad. What happened to you?"

"So you've moved in here, the two of you, in other words?"

"Nothing gets past you."

"You couldn't have told me this?"

"You're rarely—what's the word I'm looking for?—*present*."

"What about that time you told me you'd lied to me about my mother's deathbed, um, stipulation that I had to live with you till you died in order to inherit the house, and you said that the reason you'd made up that lie was that you wanted me to keep living with you because you liked having me around?"

"Well I don't remember the conversation you allude to and in any case you're twenty-six, do you expect me to continue raising you indefinitely?"

"Raising me? More like sinking me. I don't need or want you around, I was just trying to get to the bottom of your hypocrisy, which, like your dickness, has none. Raising me. I'm an adult, thank you very much, with a job."

"That's not a job, it's an abdication. You, with your aptitude for math, could have been a millionaire by now, but you're not one. You know why? Because you fail to recognize that the purpose of math is not math, the purpose of math is counting, and counting is an act of aggression, and you, who are not devoid of aggression, fail to locate or understand it in yourself or in the world. Being alive is a rough business and counting knows this. When you put them to use on people and things—and why else would they exist?—the basic mathematical operations are crimes. Addition is theft, subtraction embezzlement, multiplication rape, division murder. You, a math teacher, have terrible thoughts you can't act on because they're all backed up in your head. So you turn them on me, the wrong person. Here's a little equation for you to consider: you don't kill someone because he insults you now and then, you kill someone because if you don't, he'll kill you.

"You and I, we should have started making money together half a dozen years ago when you graduated from college, when your math skills were sharpest and my acumen and energy had not waned as they now have. Instead, you moped around the house, unreachable, because of I don't know what, the death of your mother five years before? And meanwhile my powers leaked away, I lost everything, we wandered like a pair of fools into the future, and you became a math teacher and tried to kill me, but all you've killed is time. Grotesque!"

"Who would like some crackers and cheese?"

The two men sat on cushioned stools at an amoeba-shaped

island in the middle of the kitchen topped with a great whorled black marble slab. Henrietta, who'd shifted the burden of her weight from her shoes to her feet, brought them their snack, which they ate. Despite the hour, she went into the next room and continued to unpack.

"I'd rather be a math teacher than be a liar who abandons one family and gloms onto another without ever telling them the first one exists."

"Admittedly not my finest hour."

"Admittedly not your finest *decade and a half*. But what do you mean, you lost everything?"

"I mean when demand for my product spiked, I borrowed from an institution that offered an interest rate lower than the belly of a pregnant ant, and I ordered three million units from a Chinese plant I had not done business with before. My Malaysian account manager had warned me against working with the Chinese manufacturer but I thought he was speaking out of soreness at me for not giving him the additional business, which he couldn't have handled anyway. The Chinese required an unusually large deposit and a swift payment schedule. Demand for my product went soft, I paid off the Chinese with the sum from the lending institution, but couldn't pay the lending institution back, and while their interest rate was low, their penalty was severe. They took my business and my house."

"They took our house?"

"Yes."

"When did this happen?"

"In the spring."

"So who owns the house?"

"Well, you do."

"I do?"

"You will."

"When?"

"When you sign the papers."

"What papers?"

"The ones my daughter hopefully at some point will give you to sign."

"What's Sylvia got to do with the house?"

"She got the lending institution to agree to deed it to you."

"How'd she do that?"

"By marrying it."

The head of his stepfather started feeling extra-real to Karl right now. It was smaller than he remembered. Surrounding the long, wispy goatee, tiny, stiff white hairs protruded from his red-gray lower face, as if the hairs were holding their ground while the face shrank to reveal them. On the sides of the upper skull the white hair was lustrous and thick, but sparse on top, where the skin was pinkish-brown. The lobey ears, more red than pink, showed veiny signs of wear, and were as if nibbled by the sun on top. When he talked his bone-white, even teeth emitted a distant whistle; Karl attempted to contemplate the totality of dental suffering in the life of Jones and failed, not for lack of imagination but for lack of desire to come face-to-face with his own oral future. Notwithstanding the compromised state of each of its parts, the head itself was an object of uncommon beauty, a brilliant modern sculpture made of little odds and ends gathered on a junkyard excursion and signifying man's struggle to make good use of his time.

"Sylvia bought you this house," Karl said.

"You're not as stupid as I thought."

"She married Stony to save her mother and father from financial ruin."

"How should I know why she married him? She didn't even tell me about it till after."

"So she'll divorce him now."

"No."

"Why not?"

"She loves him."

"No she doesn't."

"Yes she does."

"Why won't she divorce him?"

"It is technically he who owns the houses, yours and mine."

"So?"

"So if she divorces him he'll sell them."

"So tell her to divorce him."

"Why should I?"

"Because she's miserably unhappy that she married him."

"You mean you are."

"Tell her to divorce him. Put your daughter's happiness before your own."

"She's twenty-nine years old, it's not my place to tell her who to divorce."

"She's twenty-nine?"

"How old did you think she was?"

"Twenty-four."

"You were wrong."

"You need to release her from the belief that only she can save you. Also, she needs guidance, and you're her father."

"She's always been independent, I raised her with a free hand."

"Look how well that turned out."

"It turned out extremely well. My daughter is a peach."

"Gentlemen." The men looked up. Henrietta stood in the doorway between the kitchen and dining room in a bright floral dress and socked feet with a shadeless table lamp in her hands. "This is our first night in our beautiful home. No yelling, please. Monty, come and play us something on the piano."

"You say no yelling but asking him to play something on the piano is the same as taking his side in the argument."

She angled her face slightly downward toward the parquet floor in order to look at him through her brow in a way he'd seen certain black women look at children and white people that said, "My patience is at an end and you'll be unable to endure the result of further resistance."

"Piano's out of tune. A truck ride is hard on an instrument of such delicacy," regardless of which Jones sat and played "Murder, He Says" while Karl rambled the emergent living room in search of objects his home had been denuded of, as if looking for the trail of crumbs leading back in time to the blight from which the whole of his life had derived. Jones played jauntily. Despite the loss of his business and the decline of his body, this was a happy moment for him. He'd reunited with his first wife, escaped the poorhouse, moved into a beautiful home. In so doing, he'd also blotted out the existence of Karl's mother. He was a pretty good piano player and Karl wondered why the assholes of the world played piano and succeeded in love and had good luck, or were tall, handsome, and strong, or received grateful oral sex from an eager older person.

"Will bring on nobody's murder but his own," Jones concluded, singing—shouting, really—only the last line of the song he'd played as was his custom. "Lyrics composed by Frank Loesser, an unhappy and productive man who chain-smoked, wrote seven hundred songs, married at age forty-nine, and was dead of lung cancer ten years after that. Did I mention I'll be teaching a finance course in the fall at the MetroTech Center just on the other side of Flatbush Avenue?"

"All right well bedtime," Henrietta said.

She had gone toward the end of the song into a room of the house beyond Karl's sight and thoughts, and appeared now framed by the doorless threshold between the foyer and the so-called music room where Karl sat on a deep, soft couch. She held a checkered blanket out to him. "You can sleep where you're sitting but you'll have to come and take the blanket from my hands because the moment in the evening has come when my feet have simply got to save themselves for the hike up the mountain to the bedroom. Next time you come we'll have a bed upstairs for you as well but you caught us unprepared this time."

Toward the end of the song, somewhere in the soft, deep couch, perhaps caused by fatigue, or by an intimation in the song, Karl ceased to be able to herd his thoughts and sensations into a fenced-in Karl type of area. Attributes and qualities—of the music, the piano, the player, the bare lightbulbs, the chairs, the boxes, the windows, the air, the hour—shook loose of the objects with which he had learned to associate them and circulated freely in the room, which is to say, in Karl. Henrietta's invitation to take the blanket from her outstretched arms therefore required an additional "Karl!" which reinstated, in a jolt, enough Karl for him to get up and walk across the room and take the blanket from her hands.

The blanket came into his arms as a delicious sort of gooey softness and lemony flavor and interconnected cluster of red and black squares. Henrietta's soft, brown, meaningful face drifted off to the side of his view and then around back of it where it wasn't properly a view anymore but a set of sounds, a smell, a feeling in his back and mind. And so he did not see but felt and heard the older couple laboriously ascend the stairs, while he looked at and through the two glass doors that were the double entrance to the house, the vestibule between them a decompression chamber between the deep sea of the world and the submarine of the home. He saw himself doubled and suspended in these two bright square diving bells, one inside the other, above the dark, blurred Brooklyn floor. Up into this double Karl of light rose a bioluminescent thing, thin, furred in phosphor, enlarging as it rose, with skinny legs and swollen lower thorax.

"Now everyone's here," Jones said. "We're already halfway up, you let her in," he directed his stepson from above.

Karl came flooding back to Karl. She wore a short white cotton dress that her thin taut legs went all the way up into and her massive belly pressed against. She kissed his cheek and whispered his name in his ear, reassembling him inside himself.

"Mom, Pops, how are you?"

"We're splendid, dear," her mother said.

"I've reached the age when I'm reduced to complicated pleasures," her father said.

There was a long hiatus in movement and sound in which each of them looked at the others and seemed to wonder who would move or speak, and hoped it would not be themselves. Old impatience—it, too, had entered through the vestibule—settled into all.

"Come on, my darling," Jones said to his child, "your mother's feet are a pair of meatloafs. I know you've got a heavy load but mount these few stairs so we don't have to go down and back up again."

She did as told with a haughty and forlorn sigh. On the fifth stair she kissed her father's elaborately sculptural head. On the seventh, she leaned out over her own belly, put her arms around her mother's upper back, and pressed her cheek to hers.

"How are you, dear?" the mother said.

"My back aches and I shit five times a day."

There was a stiffness of bodies as they pulled away caused neither by the daughter's advanced gestation of the grandchild nor by the grandma's swollen feet and fatigue at midnight of moving day. Everyone waited again for someone to act, the family of three-and-a-half of blood on the stairs and the one by a thread at the foot of them. "The blankets are in a box in the dining room as the young man can tell you, please understand," Henrietta finally said. Sylvia navigated around her parents' forms and back down the stairs with the sullenness that expressed itself so fully in the lowered and turned-in shoulders of thin girls, even pregnant ones.

She faced Karl and put her hands on her hips and raised one side of her mouth in a kind of facial tic Karl interpreted as *Well, family, you know?* "You want to show me the box with the blankets?" she said.

He put the soft wool one Henrietta had handed him around her goosebumped shoulders and arms and burnished it onto her skin with the palms of his hands and held it in place with them.

"Good night, kids," said the tired mother, and crept up one more stair, and one more. "Let's have a big breakfast tomorrow, I'll make it for us after we all sleep well," she said, covering the next ten hours with the warm blanket of a happy wish, and the older folks went up, and the younger ones wondered at each other in the lit-up downstairs.

"Is it because of her pride?" Karl asked.

"What?"

"Or is it that you didn't invite her to your wedding? Or had the wedding to begin with?"

"I've just had a long drive, preceded by a horrible day."

"Oh yeah, that brunch."

"*After* the brunch."

"What happened after the brunch?"

"He . . . Picture an hour alone with that man, as his wife."

"I'd rather not."

"What do you mean, pride?"

"That she loves the house you gave her but isn't the kind of person who can just accept a free house from her daughter without feeling her dignity has been compromised."

"Remember when you met me and thought I was a burglar?"

"You mean because you told me you were one?"

"The relationship between me being a burglar and what I actually was is about the same as the relationship between what you perceive is going on between my mother and me right now and what is actually going on between her and me."

"So what actually were you?"

"For real, Karl."

"Oh, for real? Hey now don't get me wrong, I'm crazy about you even if you don't turn out to actually like me, which I still can't tell if you even really do, but 'for real' is exactly what you were not on the day we met, and haven't been since."

Her eyes grew moist and she trembled. Her flesh, generally taut and athletic and gripping the air, now was passive and slack. "Well I still don't even believe people do things for the reasons they announce they're doing them for but I'm mad at my mother, Karl, for taking back that white asshole who threw his nigger family in the garbage and bought himself a brand-new white one with his new money he got on the backs of some other dollar-a-day niggers in Asia. And I'm mad at *him* because, well, that. Imagine for just one second what happens to a teenage girl who looks like me when she has to move from Centraldale to the Hart Crane Projects."

"So this is the same nigger—"

"Careful!"

"—and white asshole you just bought a house for by marrying a second white asshole who took the first asshole's house away from him?"

"Don't let anyone say I'm not a loyal daughter."

He guided her by the blanket he was still touching her through over to the couch in the music room and tried to push her down gently onto it. She tensed up. He kissed her cheek. She groaned and sat down on the couch.

"Let's talk for a minute and then go to sleep," he said. "I can be on the floor here next to you. I'd like to wake up and see you first thing, that would be amazing. Before we have the breakfast here your mother wants to make, let's sneak out and have a cup of tea, the two of us, in a little diner, it would be nice just to sit with you somewhere."

He watched a strange convulsing of this body that had become dear to him, a wrinkling, reddening, moistening, swelling, and opening up of the beautiful face.

"Please tell me what's wrong," he said.

"It's intolerable. You can't imagine."

"I was made to imagine."

"No, no, no, you don't know, you're too innocent, you can't know, it's horrible, it's horrible, I can't stand it much longer!"

She wept in drawn-out moans and gasps he felt in his legs and chest. He held her hand and stroked her creamy inner forearm. After a time, she seemed to have temporarily exhausted her distress, and stared idly at the wall across from her through wet eyelashes while he stared at her staring. It occurred to him to cheer her up with an anecdote about a man she disliked that might make him more sympathetic to her.

"So I found out something interesting about Arv and those high school boys."

"Did Arv tell you? I'll kill him!"

"Why would you kill him? And no, he didn't tell me, he didn't have to. Are you really so opposed to Arv that you don't find his behavior the slightest bit charming?"

"Oh, I'm so relieved you think it's charming."

"Why relieved?"

"I was sure you'd be really mad at me, if you found out. I hoped you'd never find out."

"Why would I be mad at *you*?"

"Because that would be a normal reaction to finding out your friend paid to have you beaten."

"What friend?"

"Me."

Karl dropped his friend's hand, stood up fast, careened forward, landed on the low wooden coffee table by the couch, smashed his shin on it. Its leg snapped off and sailed across the room. Shin pain came in swift, sharp bursts.

Movement from above. "What's going on down there?"

"Nothing!"

Swollen feet lingered on the landing and, satisfied their own treacherous journey down and eventually back up the stairs could in no way ameliorate the calamity in the music room, retreated.

"What *are* you?" Karl said. He tried to stand. The floor surged up toward his face. He stopped it with his hands, at some cost to them. He had lost track of where he was in relation to the room and to his body and to hers. He looked around for her, found her legs, stared at them in woe.

"Karl, I'm so sorry, please forgive me, I need you to."

Outrage combined in him with a recognition of his momentary strategic advantage. "I need you not to have hired people to hurt me and then lie to me about it. Why did you do it?"

"I was desperate. He had threatened to take the house, to take everything, to ruin my father. I blackmailed Arv."

"Well, fine. Who wouldn't? But why exactly did you blackmail him to have me beaten up by two boys?"

"I was desperate!"

"To do what?"

"I thought if you would get hurt—just a little bit!—and then I was there to take care of you, and then convince you Stony was behind it, I could—this won't sound good—soften you up."

"For *what*?"

"For something I figured out once I met you that you were totally unsuited for. But I find you help me in this totally other unexpected way."

"What on earth way is that?"

"By being this innocent, adorable, melancholy weirdo who's just himself, who isn't machinating or striving, who wants nothing more than to carry on with his unambitious, unremarkable life— I've never met anyone like you."

"Oh please, stop, you're overwhelming me with flattery!"

"Though I admit it's not been easy to adore you when being adored seems to make you so uncomfortable."

"Yes, you're right, that's true, I don't so much like being adored when the adoration is expressed through secrecy, lying, and having the shit beaten out of me."

If someone who knew nothing about these two were to have wandered into this harshly lit, not-yet-assembled room of this Brooklyn house on this, the darkest night of the season, and seen the man on his knees before the strangely thin pregnant female who was seated above him and leaning down toward him, that person might have been excused for believing the man was begging for mercy from this troubled goddess of uncertain function, and that the goddess was lamenting that mercy was not hers to dispense.

"If I had known you then, I never would have done it."

"How reassuring," he said, put his hands gently on her alabaster knees, and caressed them, not in affection but in one final, small expenditure of a lust that would never be fully expressed. "And I guess it was you and not Arv who gave me the roofie at that party?"

"No, I think you just passed out, Karl." She looked down at his hands on her knees. "So are you still my friend then?" she asked.

"You told me Stony had me beaten because he knew you had a crush on me. That's three lies in one, none of which you can even explain. How am I to believe anything you say or do now? You hug me, you kiss me, you claim to care for me, and all the while you probably are out to hurt me again, only worse this time, for reasons that are beyond the comprehension of this person who was 'totally unsuited' for whatever psychotic activity you 'softened him up' to help you with. Am I still your friend? I haven't ever been your friend, I've been your puppet. I can't tell you how much I wish I could go back to the tolerable misery of not ever having known you. Since I cannot, I will do the second-best thing, which is never to see you again."

"No! I won't allow it!"

"You just keep the fuck away from me or I'll call the cops."

He was on his feet now, wobbling, trying not to look at her face, because he had in fact looked at it for an instant, and did not want to know that this face he had loved could look like this, that any face could, and so he looked at the window behind the couch and saw the shambling figure who shimmered there on the brink of dissolution. "I have done everything you asked of me," he said. "I have granted all the favors I was capable of. Now I ask you not to seek me out, not to try to persuade me of anything or comfort me or help me or befriend me. Leave me alone, now and forever."

"No, Karl. You can't do this. I love you!"

On wavy, distant feet, he ran out of the house and into the hot air. He doubted on the short flight of stone stairs from house to stunted yard that his feet, if they could get him to his car, would endure for long enough to press the car's pedals all the way out to the town on Long Island that was presumably his home, and so he made the choice to pass out in the soft dirt beneath the yard's magnolia tree, and had lain down there, and closed his eyes, and was more than halfway to being beautifully unconscious when he heard that voice again—"Karl! Please!"—and rather than allow himself to be pierced by it or its owner repeatedly, unceasingly, fatally, he stood up and ran to his car and got in it and drove to Long Island with strength borrowed from reserves that were themselves borrowed.

But it was not just a matter of driving to Long Island, not when the Brooklyn-Queens Expressway so resembled his mind. Monstrous entities, far larger than himself, roaring, surged up from the dark and would have crushed him had he not swerved to the brink of a steep drop down to his own annihilation, guarded only by a barrier his former trust in the solidity of which he now saw as deluded and pathetic. Meanwhile the road—rough, marred, exhausted—kept on beneath him, but tenuously, on the point of ceasing to be. The Kosciuszko Bridge, that promising but ultimately sad affair that delivered a man from one borough to the next, came and went. The tops of warehouses, shops, offices, industrial places of business, homes, dark and quiet—in which no one could be happy for long—rushed past him uttering low and even whispers in a language whose each sound was indistinguishable from every other sound.

And so out of Brooklyn and Queens and onto Long Island proper on that pathway to the sea, the LIE. Here another problem beset Karl whose origin and meaning he almost understood in the same way he was almost a contented person with consistently good luck. It was the problem of the headlights, a single pair, stronger than his and higher off the ground. It happened all the time of course on this and other roads, even in the black hours of the night when so few cars were out: two souls went the same way for miles—how many ways were there? How many roads on this narrow landmass could speed a soul from west to east with minimum effort and maximum expediency? And yet one could not discount its insistence, sometimes twenty yards back, sometimes fifty, never more than a hundred. When he went left, it went left; when he went right, it did. He slowed down, it slowed down; he sped up, it did. It bugged him. It plagued him. Exhausted though he was and in danger of losing control of his vehicle even on this no-brainer of a road, he passed his own exit to shake it loose, and did not shake it loose, this pair of lights which, sometime around

Ronkonkoma, he understood to be the mistake he had made in the spring, the one that had led inevitably to that other mistake, and that other one, and that other one, and to say that it was following him was to understate and therefore was probably not so different from saying that the ass of a man followed his dick, except when he was standing still, or backing up, or jumping down or diving down a deep dark hole.

He pulled a U-y in one of those places you're not supposed to pull one, a curved dirt path across the verdant meridian—an interstate's casual nod to what preceded it—and hurried to return to the place he could no longer regard as home, and did not so long as he was on that highway look back once to find out if that thing was still with him. But he did look back when he got off of it because he knew that no amount of not looking back would make the thing not be there, and not only was it there but so was another thing, and he knew what the first thing was and he knew what the second was even if he didn't know or didn't want to think he knew how the second, the husband, had found the first, the wife.

And it loomed before him, the pale façade of that thing he had lived in all his life and would now leave, though leaving was a country occupied by murderers and thieves. Each stair hurt the foot that touched it. The sad old faux wood paneling would have baked and crumbled to the rug in blackened shards had the rays from his eyes been as corrosive as the memories that rode out on them and touched all he saw. His bed, that sagging coffin draped in smelly cloth, accepted him, and he accepted it, for now.

But what kind of prig would not take a beat-down from the girl he loved? And if she was coming to do him harm, or her husband was, or they both were, for reasons he couldn't begin to understand or give a crap about, how was that worse than the life he would have if they did not? These were the questions he awoke to, posed, it seemed, by the dim predawn light. In the three hours since he'd come home, someone had plastered him to his bed. Someone had replaced the feeling in his limbs with a buzzing noise. Someone had narrowed the tube of his throat. Someone had gently laid an anvil on his face. It was himself who had done this. In short order he'd made a cohesive agglomeration of life-squandering mistakes, the first being to have met her, the last being to have shunned her. His life had been a series of slow, dull shoves through time toward the grave, which she had disrupted by existing in proximity to him, and now the sun was coming up on a post-Vetch life that was pathetic, intolerable, and that he could have prevented just by forgiving her—or even not forgiving her but living with her in unforgiveness and accepting the beating and any subsequent treacheries and lies as the modest price of loving and being loved, which was what he assumed most couples did.

Dark blond hair greased and matted, shirt and socks ripe, skin oiled by summer neglect, eyes red, mouth a bog, he went once more to the Volvo that was as many Volvos as there were times of day, and drove off to find her, late for a happy outcome though this action no doubt was. He went to her matrimonial home, where the chain was up in the gap in the high stone wall at the bottom of the drive. He parked the car and cut across the lawn on foot, stiff pants chafing his thighs. Something here was wrong. No cars were parked in the turnaround. The garage doors were shut and locked. Shutters he'd not seen before sealed windows through which, had they not been blocked, one could have seen the windows at the back, through which one could have seen the cove far off and small. There was about the place a cold gray feel despite the hot and fuggy August air. He pressed the bell, knocked on panes, went around the back and found the Stoningtons gone, what invert life the place possessed quenched.

He went back to the elaborate shack where she and her friends had lived, whose kitchen he'd attempted to help her clean, where his soft and beautiful yellow hat—that daffodil among head coverings—had been taken from him: a sore spot in the world, though if oneself is sore then everywhere one goes is sore.

A look in the window revealed a single damaged chair, a broom, a mop, stray papers, bits of plastic jetsam, dust, grime. A few objects remained on the porch as well: cardboard boxes that looked full of someone's stuff, an old gray vinyl suitcase, a gray wool blanket with a lump beneath. The lump was Arv, who stirred: "Oh, hey."

"What happened?"

"Stony sold the place," Arv said, still supine, his gluey face emerging from the top of the blanket. "We all have had to move, just as well, weirdest place I've ever lived, all those straight girls from the beach with no feel for hygiene, a few memorable parties though." Arv sat up, threw the blanket off, leaned against the house's chipped green front wall. He had the look of an old sailor now, tanned, lean, in his pleasantly worn T-shirt with horizontal red and white stripes, dark hair lightly rimed with ocean salt, putty face arranged in quiet lumps of dignified sadness. "I'm just wait-ing here with the last of my crap for the guys to pick me up, not expecting them for a few more hours, teenagers need a lot of sleep."

"Where's Stony?"

"How should I know?"

"Where's Sylvia?"

Arv shrugged.

"I screwed things up with her."

"How?"

Karl told him.

"Oh, yeah, sorry about that."

"Why didn't you tell me she did that?"

"I did tell you, indirectly."

"Why not directly?"

"Because I'd've been scared to death of the consequences."

"Which would've been what?"

"How dense exactly are you?"

"Pretty dense."

"Still, I regret doing that."

"Don't worry, it doesn't matter."

"That's a start."

"A start to what?"

"To all the things I wish I hadn't done not mattering."

"So you don't know where Sylvia is?"

"Still don't."

"Where would you look?"

"I wouldn't look anywhere. I would leave town and never come back. That is one terrifying chick. She hates men, especially white men. Can't you see she's playing you and Stony off each other? She'll do anything. Hey, I found a sweet little apartment above the hardware store, free screws. You should come over when I have it fixed up."

"Thanks."

"Or we'll come by your place one night with weed, cheer you up."

Though he knew it would be closed, Karl tried the bar he'd danced in with her, and drank in with her, and told her he'd killed her father before he'd known that was her father and before he'd known he hadn't killed him, to which she'd reacted—corroborating what Arv had just said about her—with insufficient chagrin. The bar was closed.

He went to the gas-station-and-café where something or other had happened, he no longer knew what, and saw Jen, that uncharted territory, manning the register as it seemed she always did, a whole life he hoped never to see into. He went home and ate cold cereal. He shot pool, lay on the couch, lay on his bed, bathed, lay on his bed, boiled eggs, ate them, spread low-fat cream cheese on a square slice of bread from a loaf he'd brought home in a plastic bag from the store. He went to the picture window at the front of his husk and he saw a car that he thought was her come down the street. It was not her. He saw a hedge that he thought was her move in a light breeze that he thought was her. A cloud that he thought was her covered the sun that he thought was her.

A woman appeared in his thoughts whom he believed to be his mother. He lay on the tan leather couch in the living room on which he'd lain while Sylvia had sat tensely drinking tea in a chair across from him on the day they met. There the two women were, one dead, the other likely not, blurred phantoms in the fictive room of his thoughts. He stood up, walked out his front door, and found not the even green yard and staid gray street but the wilderness in which he'd joined his sweetheart on her honeymoon, only more wild, with a less clear pathway through it and more brambles to be stung by. He came to a stand of light small trees and peered into their midst. His mother was enfenced by them, wrapped by vines, partially obscured from sight by them, stuck. The trees, he discovered, as he drew closer, did not prevent her from moving, a set of antlers did—it was they that had stuck her. They were attached to a thing, a living thing, a stag, he guessed—though he was from the suburbs and did not know the names of horned woodland things—covered in thick and luxuriant black fur. Its eyes were of a pale and eerie blue, an inhuman frequency of light that represented capacities and impulses beyond the control of a civilized cortex. This thing that could not be reasoned with lay on the forest floor with his mother and embraced her, inside an impenetrable fence of trees. The red embroidery in the white peasant blouse, he'd half known all along, was not embroidery but blood. One of the stag's dark antlers was piercing his mother's chest. The muscular animal jerked violently and drove its antler deeper into her flesh. She looked at her son calmly and said, "Well, I guess you had to know sometime."

He was halfway to the kitchen with desiccated mouth when the doorbell rang. As proposed, Arv arrived with his young friends and the weed, the former self-evident, the latter announced. Karl saw that it was nighttime and felt through the open door that the heat, by which he'd been untouched when the door was closed, had not abated.

"I don't mean to be rude but I've got to get some water," he said over his shoulder on his way to the kitchen.

"Cotton mouth!" Paul said behind him, or Hal.

Alone by the fridge, he glanced up and caught his second, blurred self on the kitchen windowpane, against the backdrop of the black air, pressing a second, blurred glass into a recess in the second, blurred fridge door, and watched himself watch the glass fill up with water from an unseen source. These figures that came and went across a home's nighttime panes were optical stand-ins for the second self the self always imposed between it and the obscured world.

When he reentered the living room the boys were in the midst of removing small glass pipes, presumably for weed, from the vo-luminous pockets on the sides of their pants legs. From one's pocket came the beautiful green weed itself in its sealed plastic sheath. "We need to put water in these," said Hal, or Paul, indicat-ing the pipes, or bongs, as they were called. "Where's your kitchen, Mr. Floor?"

"If you don't know where my kitchen is then you've haven't been making yourself as at home here as I thought."

The guys made a certain kind of slowed-down "Huh-huh-huh" sound that meant they were giggling and also was a sign that they were a certain kind of teenage boy, a mating call if you will to other boys of their ilk—not in the *Let's give each other blow jobs* sense of mating but in the *Let's skateboard* or indeed the *Let's smoke weed* sense—and a non–mating call to people not of their ilk as if to say, *This giggle is way more nuanced than you think even though it might sound dumb to you which if it does sound dumb to you then you're not one of us.*

"Got any food?" one of them said.

"Not much. Some cream cheese. Knock yourself out."

They went to the kitchen to fill their bongs and explore the fridge. Karl sat heavily on the upholstered comfy chair.

"I know this is going to end very badly for me," Arv said, easing himself down onto the couch, "so you don't even have to say it."

"Okay, I won't," Karl said by rote.

"You all right, buddy?"

"I'm fine." He was not.

"We're here to cheer you up, man. The boys like you. They feel they owe you."

"That's sweet," Karl said. He meant it, to the extent he could

mean anything that was not relevant to the central and only purpose for which he now drew breath.

"Mr. Floor!" they said, reentering, arms loaded with filled bongs,
cream cheese, white bread, olives, Sunny Bonghit fruit-flavored drink
snack, and prune juice. "Are you constipated?"

"My stepfather is."

"Oh yeah, that dude who we did some work in his yard."

"That dude's yard is my yard too."

"Are you totally going to get high with us, Mr. Floor?"

"I doubt it."

"Mind if we do?"

"At this point I doubt I could estimate exactly how very much
I don't give a flying fuck at a rolling doughnut what you do."

They'd already, it turned out, loaded their bongs, and during
Karl's assertion of emphatic indifference, clinked them together in
a toast, held flames to them, inhaled enormous amounts of mari-
juana smoke, held it in their lungs for a while, and, shortly after
Karl had concluded his peroration, repeated the deadpan machine-
gun laugh, now doubling as an exhalation of pot smoke. The boys
looked at each other with eyes made "Chinese," as they would
have said if they could talk now, and made a sound the person of
discernment will notice is slightly different from both the regular
giggle and from the pot-exhalation giggle—more of a whispered,
guttural "Haw-haw-haw" this time, which, if translated into words
they could not say because, again, they could not talk right now,
might've been, "We've toasted, and now we're toasted."

Arv, who sat at the end of the tan leather couch closest to Karl
in his chair, nudged Hal, who sat in the middle, which in turn jostled Paul, who sat at the other end—unless it was Paul he'd

nudged, and Hal who'd been jostled—and made a friendly but curt and firm head motion toward Karl, as if to say, "This is the part we rehearsed, boys, come on."

"Okay, okay, we have a thing to say to you, Mr. Floor," said the one whom we must now call Paul and leave it at that to conserve energy. "It's, like, how sorry we are about punching you last spring. It was a really sucky thing to do, we didn't want to, but we needed the money, and Mr. Pepper can be really convincing, but now he's sorry too, and we're sorry too."

Karl felt Paul had called Arv "Mr. Pepper" not because he would ordinarily refer to him with that honorific but because Paul felt using it would be a sign of respect for Mr. Floor, and Karl was touched by this, a little bit.

"That was a beautiful speech and I accept your apology."

At this news Paul and Hal enthusiastically high-fived each other and relit their bongs and redoubled their stonedness. Arv nudged Paul once more, this time to signal he'd like to be passed one of the bongs.

"You don't mind, do you?" Arv asked Karl.

"Let's see," Karl said, "you've hired these seventeen-year-olds to beat me up, you've broken into my house and fellated them in my basement, they've just now filled the air of my living room with pot smoke, and I don't mind any of these things, but yes, I mind *this*."

Hal said, "Mr. Floor, that's how come your trig class was so fun, 'cause you crack these weird hostile jokes like you hate everyone even though we can tell you really love everyone but you're just really lonely and sad."

Hal's stoned acuity and tenderness consoled Karl in the modest way one can be consoled who is inconsolable.

"Looks like we have to repeat senior year," Paul said. "Hey, maybe we can take trig with you again."

"And we brought you a mixtape," Hal said, and pulled a CD from the leg of his cargo pants that had the imaginative title *Mixtape for Mr. Floor.*

Karl pointed languidly to the home entertainment center Jones must have left behind not out of respect for Karl's desire to be entertained but because Henrietta had a better one.

A reggae song came loudly from the speakers and its beat made time lurch awkwardly forward, which reinforced the experience of time Karl was already having, and enlarged his susceptibility— scant though it was in this difficult period—to the music's beauty.

Hal, having started the machine, danced jerkily to the middle of the room, not at all in time to the song. His indifference to the song's time was his youthful body's way of asserting its indifference to time itself. For his little hayloft of blond hair, for his stoned red eyes and smooth skin, his dirty T-shirt and unfatted torso, his too-low pants with ragged cuffs, his dirty sneakers slapping randomly against the rug, how could Karl not have envied him? How could Karl's sense of loss, of the irreversible departure of vital energies, of the finality of the past, and of the future, not have sharpened?

Hal's two friends were on their feet now too. A song played that went, "If you come from Brooklyn, and if you come from Queens, and if you come from Centraldale you're an African . . .'Cause if you come from Seacrest, and if you come from Levittown, and if you come from Ronkonkoma you're an African."

Karl, on the chair, asked Arv, hopping on the rug, "Why are you scared of her? Seems to me Stony's the scary one."

"He's scary too, but at least with him you know what you're getting up front."

"You think she's out to harm me?"

"Yes!"

"Why?"

"Karl, do I look like a guy who understands women?"

The three friends danced in a slow and tightening circle, holding hands, laughing, making googly eyes at one another, sportsworn sneakers rising and falling higgledy-piggledy. They mewed, purred, nuzzled, the circle tightened, their hands went to each other's arms and necks. When the circle stopped spinning, and they went from dancing to swaying, and their three faces touched and did not seem to be about to separate, Karl climbed the stairs and went to bed, his default response for twenty-six years.

The noises awakened him. He could not locate their source. He looked at his slick brown walls, his art and music posters, his chair and desk, his closet door, the plastic pull-down window shades of a color adjectivized by the saleswoman at the five-and-dime as *aubergine*. The noises, made in part by human voices, he thought, increased in volume and speed. He took a long look at all the things that would not be the same or would not exist once the noises stopped. There was the light itself, too, the main and first one, pink-hued, hardly detectable suburban predawn light to look at and to say good-bye to at least his current understanding of, and then the unintelligible sounds again, which he thought included shouting. He was up out of bed, always clothed these days, indifferent to the wash of hours, and he was at his window, drawing up its shade, and looking out upon his moist and near-dark lawn, up which two tall, thin, shadowed figures, male and female, advanced toward the house. Was one behind the other? They merged and came apart and merged again, and whispered or grunted. They disappeared under the eave beneath him. He'd left the window open for a little unconditioned air to sleep by, and now he slammed it shut so he wouldn't have to hear the sounds that came from the figures below. He went to the little bed he'd outgrown and got into it one last time. He pulled the thinned, drab, Karlesque sheet above his head in a last vestigial attempt not to know. But he was already on the stairs when the banging on the door began. The door was hit at least ten times. He opened it—why try to avoid something that might as well already have happened?

"There's this thing, it's called a doorbell, maybe you've heard of it."

"I haven't."

She was wet and breathing hard, her breasts and belly enormous in her pink stretch skirt and black T-shirt with the PARTY TILL HE'S CUTE epigram. There was some other oddness about her too, and her husband was not in sight.

He felt the foyer wall with his palm, behind his back, the grainy consistency of the matte white paint and the plaster beneath it impressing themselves on his skin, which interested him greatly. *So this, in the end, is the foyer wall.*

"Let's get away from the door," she said.

He wanted to jump, but made himself walk calmly to the living room and stand in its center, on its soft Persian rug. She joined him there. The door remained open.

He saw movement at the door, but she had already said, "Karl, look at me."

He did. She was holding out his yellow hat. He took it from her hand, saw that she was holding something else, retreated several paces toward the couch, inspected his hat: still beautifully faded, yellow, soft, versatile. He raised it to his face to smell, and saw the stain.

"What is *this*?"

"You know what it is."

"I can't believe you got me back my hat."

"Hat and house."

"I don't want the house. You have the house. You earned it. I love you, even if—"

"Look at me, Karl."

He looked at her, at the thing in her hand, at the fresh stains in her hair and on her face and neck and shirt and arm. He said, "Come here close to me now." She did. "I'll take care of that," he said.

She slowly raised her thin white arms. He pulled the shirt above her head and past the thing in her hand. She was naked to the waist. Her breasts had swollen up to twice the size they'd been last spring. Light blue veins ran like subterranean springs beneath their skin and the taut skin of her round abdomen, implying the secret web of life within. He tried to clean her face with her shirt but only smeared it. He dropped the shirt and pulled her gently to him.

"Whose blood is it?"

"You know."

"Say it."

"You're somebody's stepfather now."

"What?"

"I've killed him—finally."

"Where?"

"There."

"Is he definitely—"

"If he isn't now he will be soon. Look."

"Oh, right. What do you mean, 'finally'? When did you—"

"Are you ever gonna kiss me, really kiss me? Oh yes, my beautiful man, oh Karl!"

"Oh Sylvia, Sylvia! Drop the knife!"

"Okay!"

ACKNOWLEDGMENTS

Thank you, Ben Adams, Kent Alexander, Michele Araujo, Michelle Blankenship, Gabriel Brownstein, Lisa Cohen, Conrad Cummings, Susan Dupré, Leslie Falk, Bram Gunther, Fawn Krieger, Neil Levi, Robin Coste Lewis, Carrie Majer, PJ Mark, David McCormick, Peter Miller, Lydia Millet, Richard Nash, Laura Phillips, Sylvie Rabineau, Allen Ross, Steve Ross, Sergio Santos, Lore Segal, Carole Sharpe, Myron Sharpe, Susanna Sharpe, Adam Simon, Kimberly Standiford, Les Standiford, Jacqueline Steiner, Lambert Strether, Bob Sullivan, Greg Villepique, Dan Wakefield

A NOTE ON THE AUTHOR

Matthew Sharpe is the author of the novels *Jamestown*, *The Sleeping Father*, and *Nothing Is Terrible*. He lives in New York City.